Time Lost

A novel by

Julie L. Casey

Time lost is never found - use it wisely.

Best wishes,

Julie L Casey

Amazing Things Press

Book design by Julie L. Casey

This book is a work of fiction. Any names, characters, or incidents are the product of the author's imagination and are used fictitiously. Any resemblance to actual events, locales, or persons, living or dead is purely coincidental.

ISBN 978-0615986944

Printed in the United States of America.

For more information, visit

www.teenagesurvivalist2.com
or
www.amazingthingspress.com

For my family
without whom survival would be pointless.

Chapter 1
Crumpled Memories

Time had always played a minor role in my life, lurking in the shadows, only bursting out to assert its pompous self-importance in the excruciatingly slow last three minutes of history class or the gut-wrenching last thirty seconds of our football game, when the other team had the ball and the chance to eek out the win. On other occasions, it would sweep events in front of it, in a hurry to get them over with and out of the way, like during our all-too-brief lunch periods or gone-in-a-flash summer vacations. But mostly, Time was something I never thought about; it was just another ever-present force like the geomagnetic field surrounding the earth. Who could have known that both those constant, universal forces could be brought to their knees in a matter of seconds by a force greater than both of them?

I can barely remember back when Time worked to my advantage, when it embraced me in its comforting arms and held my hand during long stretches of happiness. I remember walking to the park every day with my mother, one hand held securely by her, the other holding onto the snack she always brought me when she picked me up from daycare after work. We'd walk slowly to the swings, while Mom would ask me about my day and laugh at the cute little things I'd say. Then we'd swing together, mom on the next swing over, her hand covering mine while I grasped the chain of my swing. She'd help me swing that way, unlike the other moms, who pushed their kids from behind. I remember thinking that she was the coolest and most beautiful mom in the world, and I the luckiest boy. I have one particular picture of her in my mind: she is leaning back in the swing, her golden hair flowing out behind her; her eyes are closed and her mouth is curved into a big smile. I'm not sure if this is a real memory of her or one I've created to cope with the loss of that happy time.

Another snapshot I guard protectively, locked away in the chest of treasured memories in my mind, is of her opening the present I gave her that last Christmas before the split. I remember my dad taking a rare break from his endless pursuit of financial success to help me find the perfect gift for her, one that I was sure would ease the tension that I could feel growing in our household. I had an idea of what I wanted to get for her. Mom was a nurse at a family clinic just a few blocks from our house in North Kansas City. She always wore a nurse's watch pin on her sweater to use when she counted a patient's heartbeat. Mom always wore a sweater over her scrubs; she was always cold, even in the summer, when she complained that the air conditioners made her feel like she was in the arctic. A few weeks before Christmas that year, her watch fob broke and she had had to carry the watch in her pocket instead of pinned to her sweater. In my still-childish, 12-year-old mind, I thought the broken watch was the source of her sadness and somehow the reason she was suddenly less available to me in the evenings, often leaving me at home alone until after dinner. Sometimes Dad would even get home before she did and I could tell it upset him that she wasn't there.

Dad took me to countless jewelry stores that Saturday before Christmas, until I finally found the perfect one: the watch face was set in a gold, heart-shaped case and suspended by a gold chain from a red, enameled bow, which had a pin on the back. As with all nurse's watch pins, the clock face was upside down so that Mom could see the second hand whizzing around while she took a patient's pulse. It was expensive—I remember Dad pulling out three hundred-dollar-bills to pay for it while he half-joked that just because my name was Benjamin didn't mean I should spend all his "Benjamins." It was the most I'd ever seen him spend on anything; I think he felt the importance of the gift, too.

On Christmas, Mom sat off by herself with a little sad smile, watching me as I excitedly opened my new Xbox 360 and several games to go with it. Then I gave her my gift. The jewelry store had wrapped the gold box with a big red bow and I had made a little card shaped like a heart with a picture of us swinging drawn on it. Mom's eyes got all teary when she saw the card and when she opened the box, she merely smiled and held it against her chest, murmuring,

— *Thank you, my sweet boy.*

It wasn't the reaction I'd hoped for. I had envisioned her exclaiming with joy and embracing Dad and me in a giant hug, but she just sat there, trying not to cry. I remember being so confused and disappointed by her reaction and when I looked at Dad, he looked sad too. I think that is when I knew our family wouldn't be together much longer. I don't know how I knew; I just did. I grew up faster that day than in all the twelve years preceding it.

After the holiday break, I was almost happy to be back at school. I was already tired of playing video games by myself all day. Sometimes, one of my friends' moms would come pick me up and take me over to their house to spend the day, but since no kids my age lived in my neighborhood, I spent most of the holidays at home alone. Back at school, at least I had people to talk to for a good chunk of the day, which was a relief, even if I had to do some homework along the way. On the bus rides home from school, though, the loneliness would begin to swell up in my chest again, especially when we passed the park filled with happy toddlers and doting mothers. Even though I was way too old to swing and hold my mom's hand, I remember thinking that I'd give away everything I owned just to be able to spend another day with her in the park, while Time looked the other way and let us be for a while.

Time was no longer good to me; when I was alone, it crept along like a slowly melting icicle, but on the rare occasions that my parents would spend time with me, always separately and desperate to win my favor, Time would flow like a raging river after the spring thaw. One bright, cold day in February, Dad moved to an apartment in the heart of Kansas City, just a few blocks from where he worked as an accountant on the 14th floor of the tallest building in Kansas City. I remember counting the floors of that building one day and discovering that it was really the 13th floor, but Dad explained that people were superstitious about the number thirteen, so they skipped it in tall buildings.

One unexpected benefit of Dad moving out was that he made a point of picking me up every weekend and actually doing things with me like playing video games and taking me out to eat. We got closer than anytime I could remember in my life, but at the expense of getting further away from Mom. Their divorce was final the summer after my 13th birthday, which is on April 13th, and I began to believe in the evil of that number. It seemed that being born on the 13th had destined me to an unlucky life. Mom seemed happier than she'd been in a long time and, for some reason that angered me. When I found out that she had been dating one of the doctors at her clinic, I was furious—how could she betray both Dad and me, choosing someone else over us.

I began to beg Dad to let me move in with him and before the next school year started, he agreed to ask Mom. She was adamantly opposed to the idea at first; I thought it was because she didn't want to look like a bad mother. I picked fights with her many times over stupid little things and at other times I was just angry and sullen. Finally, she reluctantly agreed, as long as Dad could arrange to drop me off and pick me up from my same school.

After I moved in with Dad, I began to see less and less of Mom. I just couldn't get over the fact that she was to blame for the breakup of our family. Even our phone conversations became strained and I began to ignore her calls when I saw her name on the caller ID. Once, when I was staying at her house on the weekend, she had her new boyfriend over to meet me and have dinner with us. I could barely be civil. If Mom deserved the blame for turning my world upside down, then this man had to be the reason she did it; he had to be more important to her than me. I was filled with anger and loathing toward him and it was all I could do to get through dinner without choking on the baseball-sized lump in my throat. I didn't see much of my Mom after that night. I made up excuses like I was staying at a friend's house or I didn't feel good, to avoid my weekends with her. I figured she'd rather spend the time with her new man anyway.

Mom and Lyle got married just before my 14th birthday, completing the misery of that unlucky year. I was forced to walk Mom down the aisle since her dad had died before I was born. I refused to say anything, though, when the minister asked, *Who gives this woman to be married to this man?*, I just let her go and went to sit down, with my eyes on the floor for the rest of the ceremony. I didn't want to add a picture of this travesty to the treasure chest of memories in my head. After the wedding, Mom moved into a nice new house with Lyle and sold our family home. Now my childhood was boxed up and stored away like the memories of my happier days.

Chapter 2
The Day Time Stopped

My 13th year was when my family fell apart, but my 14th year was when my whole world, or more precisely, *the* whole world, collapsed. I had thought 13 was the unlucky number, the year that Time turned its back on me, but I was wrong; that year, it was I who had turned my back on Time. The following year, Time was turned back for everyone.

The August of my 14th year, I started high school at a charter school a couple of miles or so from our apartment and rode the school bus every day, which I despised. Dad promised that he would buy me a car when I turned 16, so I wouldn't have to ride the bus anymore, but that was still a year and a half away. As usual, I didn't like school much, except that I had made the Freshman Football team, not because of size, but because of speed. I liked football, mostly because it gave me something to do after school while Dad was still at work and it meant I didn't have to ride the bus back home. Dad would pick me up at 5:30, after practice, and we would grab a bite to eat before he took me home and went back to the office for a couple more hours of work. Mom tried repeatedly to get me to come to her house when Dad worked late, but I always made excuses to avoid it.

On Monday nights, Mom and Lyle would come out and watch me play in the Junior Varsity games. They'd sit by Dad and they'd all three talk civilly to each other and cheer me on. It felt so weird seeing them together like that. I wished Mom wouldn't come; then I wouldn't be forced to pretend to be happy to see her or to let her hug me after the game. I wouldn't have to shake Lyle's hand and pretend I didn't want to tackle him to the ground and pummel his face in front of all my teammates. But Time chose to make those moments stretch out uncomfortably long, so I'd try to hurry into the locker room after the game without seeing them. I'd be the last one out, hoping they'd already be gone. Sometimes they were, gratefully, but then I risked making Dad mad with my tardiness. Either way, I felt I couldn't get a grasp on Time, to use it to my advantage.

On November 1st, school started just like any other day. I rode the bus to school and spent the extra few minutes before the first bell talking with my buddies and teasing some of the freshman cheerleaders. Football season was almost over and we were talking about whether we were going to try out for basketball or wrestling. I was leaning toward wrestling because it meant lots of out-of-town weekend tournaments, but most of my friends were going out for basketball. It didn't matter. I knew that Lyle was on call most weekends and that Mom and he wouldn't be able to come to most of my tournaments, so that made it worth choosing wrestling.

Time plodded along at its normal dull pace until lunch hour. Just as I was sitting down with my tray of barely edible cafeteria food, the lights began to flicker, then went out altogether. The cafeteria was in the basement of the school, and except for the emergency exit signs, it was pitch dark. Several girls screamed and someone dropped their tray of food. There was a stunned silence for a few seconds, then the vice principal came in to usher us all up the stairs and out the doors. A couple of hundred students from other lunch periods were already outside the building, but were trying to get back in for some reason. It was chaos, and I couldn't see anything over the much taller students around me. Amid the noise and confusion of panicking students, I thought I could hear pops outside like gunfire, then an explosion and hundreds of sirens. Coach showed up then with a handheld loudspeaker and started calling out instructions in a voice that I could tell he was straining to keep calm, while telling all of us to remain calm. It was already too late for that, though.

Eventually, Coach and the vice principal got us back to our homerooms, which lined the outside of the building and had windows for light, where we waited to hear what was going on. From the windows, we could see the tops of some power poles on fire, street lights out, and dozens of cars stalled on the street below. Our teacher, Mr. Heim, just let us talk and look out the windows for almost an hour until the principal came in to explain what had happened.

— *The whole city is without power. A massive coronal mass ejection, known as a CME, from the sun has hit the earth and taken down the power grid. We've been instructed by the police department to keep you here until your parents can come pick you up.*

We didn't really understand a word that he said except that we were without power and that it was going to be awhile before it was back on. Mr. Heim allowed us to try to call our parents on our cell phones, even though we weren't supposed to have them in class. No one could get a signal and several of the phones appeared to be completely dead for some reason.

Outside, we could see people streaming out of the apartment building across the street and heard one lady shouting hysterically that her son was trapped inside the elevator and needed help getting out. I instantly started worrying about my dad being stuck on the 13th floor of his office building downtown, but there was no way I could contact him. That fact made me feel helpless and alone, even though I was in a room of 28 other people. I could tell that other people were affected by it, too, because they started trying to make calls on their cell phones again, even though we knew there was no service.

I was standing near the teacher's desk at the front of the classroom when I noticed Mr. Heim messing with his watch. He had it off his wrist and kept tapping the face of it, then holding it up to his ear, and tapping it again. When he noticed me watching him, he looked a little embarrassed.

— *It stopped working. It's an atomic watch and I guess it can't find the signal to reset itself. It must have something to do with the... thingy, you know, the corona thingy.*

Mr. Heim chuckled when he saw my dubious expression and explained,

— *I'm an English teacher; what do I know about science?*

Just then I remembered that the nurse's watch that I had given Mom for Christmas almost two years ago was an atomic watch as well. For one brief instant, I felt an enormous surge of love and concern for Mom, something I hadn't felt in a long time. I know it must've shown on my face, so I turned away quickly and looked out the window, while I struggled to stuff those feelings back into the chest of memories in my mind. I was certainly not ready to let Mom off the hook for what she did to Dad and me. Instead, I forcibly turned my feelings and my worries toward my Dad who I felt was alone and vulnerable. I worried about Dad the rest of that long afternoon that we were stuck in the school.

Several of the older students who either had cars or could ride with other students were allowed to leave, but the school held on to those of us who were under 16 until our parents or another trusted adult could come pick us up. Some of us waited a long time, in fact it was getting dark outside by the time my dad finally showed up. He was on foot, having walked the twenty-two blocks from his office building. He told me we would have to walk home, because his car wouldn't start and even if it did, he couldn't get it out of the office building's underground lot.

While we walked the fifteen blocks home, Dad told me about all the problems in his office building. The first problem was all the people that were stuck in the elevators. Dad wasn't one of them, thankfully, but he had stayed to help those that were climb up out of the hatch at the top of the elevator cars and up the ladder on the side of the elevator shaft to the floor above where it had stopped. Then everyone had to walk down the thirteen flights of stairs to street level.

As we walked, there were still tons of sirens and police cars, ambulances, and fire

15

trucks whizzing by every which way. We could see huge plumes of thick black smoke coming from several different locations in the distance. Dad said he had tried to call Mom to check on her, but couldn't get a signal, and that made my stomach do a flip-flop. I wasn't sure what upset me most: not knowing if Mom was okay, or that Dad was still concerned about her. Maybe he was just calling her for my sake, but in either case, I just looked away and changed the subject.

Chapter 3
The First Days

That night in our apartment was long and boring. We could see from the windows of our third floor apartment that the only lights on in the city belonged to the hospitals, which were no doubt being supplied by backup generators. Even then, though, most of the rooms were dark early in the evening and the lights that were on were quite dim, probably to save generator fuel. We still didn't know much about what had happened, but there were lots of rumors and, of course, conspiracy theories of some covert plan to overthrow the government flying around. I tried to tell people what the principal had told us about the coronal mass ejection, but they just answered,

— *Of course that's what they'd tell us.*

The first few days, Dad and I survived pretty well. There was still plenty of water stored in the water towers, although the mayor issued a statement, carried door-to-door by policemen and other government officials, that we should conserve water as much as possible, boil the water from the taps, and use any bottled water we had to save water for fighting fires. The messengers also told us that martial law had been declared and that the official cause of the blackout was indeed a CME, and that it had caused quite a bit of damage to the power grid, resulting in widespread outages across the country that would probably take weeks to fix. They told us that we should stock up on food and water, if at all possible.

Dad and I tried to go to the neighborhood stores to buy food and other supplies, but they were closed. Without electricity, they couldn't run their cash registers or provide lighting for their customers. After the first couple of days, some storeowners had even gone so far as to board up their windows to prevent looting. The Red Cross set up mobile stations to give out food and water. We were okay, water-wise, because Dad was a bottled water freak and had several cases of it in the pantry, but we didn't have much food since we mostly ate out. We had some boxes of cereal and Pop Tarts along with bags of chips and crackers that got us through the first few days. I was happy with eating all that junk food the first couple of days, but it soon got old and my stomach started hurting. I longed for some meat and, believe it or not, I started craving vegetables. It's funny how you want something that you never liked before just because you can't have it. I think my body knew it was missing some vital nutrients and so it was craving healthier food. We were able to get some hot meals from the Red Cross station for the first few days.

I was so bored. With no electricity, there just wasn't that much to do. I wanted to go hang out with some friends on the street, but Dad thought it was too dangerous. There were a lot of thugs walking around breaking into stores, beating and robbing people, and causing all kinds of trouble. So we just stayed in the apartment most of the time. Occasionally, we would venture out together and just walk around the neighborhood, talking to people on the streets, but we'd head back home at the sound of trouble, like sirens or shouting. In our apartment, we read lots of books, magazines, and even the school textbooks I had brought home, and played cards by candlelight in the evenings. Most nights we'd sit outside on our little balcony, trying to make out the looming, hulking shapes of buildings, trees, and stalled cars, in the dark. It was eerie not knowing what was out there. We were so used to the city being lit up at night, that it felt like we were on an alien planet. Another thing that made the city seem alien for the first few nights was the strange green, and sometimes purplish-pink light of the aurora borealis dancing in the northern sky. Our balcony faced west so we could see the aurora and the eerie reflection of it on the buildings and in the car windows on the street below. Some people feared an alien invasion that first night, but soon science and knowledge prevailed to set their fears at ease.

Time ceased to exist. The days melted into nights, which then became day again— the same day as before, it seemed. We quickly lost track of what day it was and even what season, since it was so nice outside. Often, I would wake up confused as to what time of year it was. I was certain it wasn't the dead of winter or the hottest part of summer, but I couldn't really tell if it was spring or fall until I got up and looked out the window at the last few brown leaves clinging to the ornamental trees on the strip of grass in front of the building across the street.

Dad kept trying to call mom until the batteries on both our cell phones gave out. He never was able to get a signal. He tried a pay phone down the street, but there was no dial tone. According to everyone on the street, there was no phone service anywhere and the only communication was by short-wave radio a few days after the CME. Long-wave radio waves were still too disrupted by the magnetic disturbance in the atmosphere to work.

After the first week without power, things started getting bad. Water was running out and there wasn't enough pressure in the towers to pump it out anymore. Emergency generators were running out of fuel, and with no way to refuel them, the lights in the hospitals got fewer and dimmer every night. The closest hospital to us, and the one whose windows we could see every night from our balcony, was the children's hospital. I started thinking about all those poor sick kids there, and what was going to happen to them. One of the kids in our school, a boy named Daniel, had been diagnosed with a brain tumor in junior high and was still undergoing radiation and chemo to get rid of it. I hoped he was far enough along in the treatment to be cured.

When I asked Dad about it, he just shook his head and looked away. He murmured something like,

— *I don't know, Ben.*

I could tell he didn't want to talk about it. What Dad did want to talk about, though, what he worried about and complained about every day, was how much money he was losing by not working and how big a loss the stock market was going to take because of this. He kept repeating those old sayings from my namesake, Benjamin Franklin, *Time is money* and *Lost time is never found again*. I got so tired of hearing about it that I finally told him to just get over it. He kind of freaked out on me then, yelling about how were we going to survive after the electricity comes back on, and how hard he's worked to get us where we were, and how he didn't want to lose our apartment and his new Lexus, etc. I knew we were all frustrated by the situation and we all reacted differently to the stress, so I just let it drop and ignored him every time he ranted about money after that. I wondered if he'd always been this uptight about making money, then it dawned on me that that was probably why he was hardly ever home when he and Mom were still married.

I stopped myself, though, before I could continue down that thought trail. Better to let all that remain locked away in my head.

Every couple of days or so, a policeman named Officer Ortiz, would come by our building and give us news and updates on the situation. After about nine days without electricity, Officer Ortiz came to tell us that stores had been ordered by the military to open their doors to the public and give away provisions. Armed troops were stationed in each store to ensure proper conduct and enforce strict rationing guidelines. Officer Ortiz encouraged people to get what they could as soon as possible. He said the government had promised the storeowners that they would be reimbursed by FEMA when the emergency was over.

Dad and I headed down to the market a few blocks from our building and waited in the long line that stretched down the block. Policemen were everywhere trying to keep people calm and orderly. After about an hour, we finally made it into the store where, sure enough, armed and uniformed soldiers stood guard near the doors. The grocer handed us a brown paper sack that was half-full of items; we didn't get to pick out what we wanted. As we were heading back to the doors to leave, one of the guards was confronting a man who was trying to force his way back into the store. The man began to yell that he didn't get what he needed and he was going back to get it. I couldn't hear what the guard was saying—he was trying to stay calm and keep the man from freaking out—but the man just got more and more frantic, yelling that he had to have ketchup or he would die. Dad looked in our sack and found a can of tomato paste. He offered it to the man and after the guard told him that was the best he was going to get, the man took it sheepishly and left, murmuring his thanks to Dad.

Outside the store we took a quick look in the sack. It contained a pound of ground cornmeal, two cans of green beans, two small cans of deviled ham, a box of trashcan liners, a can of V8, and a canister of salt. I was hoping for some toilet paper, as we had been out for two days and I couldn't imagine what we were going to use instead. We were feeling pretty gross by then anyway. We hadn't had a shower or bath in over a week and though we used a little water on a cloth to wipe the sweat off our bodies, we didn't dare waste enough of it to wash our hair. The toilets had become a problem, too. With the decrease in water pressure, the toilets didn't have enough water to flush. It was a good thing that we weren't eating very much or else it would've been really nasty.

The next day, the army brought in big trucks full of water and food from the USDA Commodities Warehouses in the huge storage caves along the banks of the Missouri River. They told people to bring buckets, bottles, jars, or whatever else they could use to carry water in. Again, we had to wait in a long line .to get our containers filled. Dad and I brought two buckets and four empty two-liter bottles, but the soldiers would only let us fill up the buckets and two bottles. We were able to get several cans of food, too. Everyone was being pretty decent and patient that first day of the food and water being brought in.

The next day, however, we were further back in the line and when it came our turn to fill our containers, the water in the tank was already low. We only got half what we had gotten the day before and a fight broke out in the line behind us. We just barely got out of the way before the last several dozen people in line rushed the truck, shoving and fighting to get the last of the water. The soldiers were trying to push everybody back, with one of the soldiers on a megaphone urging everybody to be calm and wait their turn. Dad and I tried to hurry away before it could get really ugly or before someone tried to steal our water. We didn't get far before we were confronted by some mean looking guys who seemed to be less interested in our water than in intimidating us.

Our water jugs were yanked out of our hands before we could even offer them to the thugs. They tossed them aside like they weren't the vital necessity that we knew they were. One ugly guy got right up in my face, took a hold of the front of my coat and pushed me back into the melee of panicked rioters. His face was so close to mine, I could smell his stinking breath and see the grainy texture of three blue tears in prison tattoo fashion staining the leathery skin at the corner of his eye. When the crowd behind me pushed me back into him, he cursed at me and punched me in the face, like he was angry that I had dared to fight back. I had been hit in the face before during football and other sports, but nothing like this. It hurt so bad that I thought I would black out. I would have fallen to the ground except for the swirling mass of turmoil pushing and bouncing me around like a buoy on turbulent waters. At that moment I understood what people meant when they say they saw stars and that the world seemed to move in slow motion for a while. Time, which had seemed non-existent for a while, now appeared like a cruelly distorted nightmare.

When I finally got my senses back, I had been deposited at the side of the crowd and I looked frantically around for Dad. I finally spotted him in the middle of the gang of thugs who were pushing him back and forth between them, each taking a crack at his face or body as he passed. I started screaming for help, suddenly realizing that the water tanker, along with the accompanying soldiers, were driving away, leaving us to fend for ourselves. After what seemed like hours of me standing by helplessly watching Dad get beat up, my nose bleeding and swelling so much I could barely see, some police officers showed up and with guns, billy clubs, and riot gear, and chased everybody off. Everybody but the few of us who were injured, that is. Dad was on his back, gasping for air like a fish out of water. An officer stooped down to check on him, but he couldn't talk to say if he was okay or not. It took a few minutes for Dad to recover enough to painfully sit up and speak again. He said he was alright, but I worried that he might have had some ribs broken because he moved gingerly for weeks afterward.

Chapter 4
Spiraling Down

*Day by day, things got progress-*ively worse. After the first few days of almost constant sirens, fewer and fewer could be heard each day. This wasn't because there were any fewer emergencies or less crime; it was because the police, fire departments, and ambulances were running out of fuel to run their vehicles. The military still had fuel in reserve, but they conserved it as much as possible. It was odd to see nothing but an occasional army Hummer on the once-busy downtown streets. Instead of sirens, more and more often we'd hear people screaming in terror or anguish, yelling for help, or crying in pain.

One old man in our building, Mr. Westcott, who had been without his oxygen for several days, collapsed and died of a heart attack—at least that's what we thought he probably died of. Dad and some of the other residents had been checking on him every day, but one morning when someone checked on him, they found him dead in his ratty, old armchair, clutching his chest but, incongruously, with a peaceful expression on his face. When I got there with Dad, the smell made my stomach heave. Dad and some of the other men took his body, wrapped it in a blanket, and carried it to the children's hospital, where at least they would have a morgue. When Dad came back, he was visibly shaken and wouldn't talk the rest of the afternoon. It made me sick to think of what he saw there, so I didn't even want to know.

I began to have nightmares at night and even some hallucinations during the day. Dad said it was probably because of the lack of adequate food and water, but I thought there was a lot more to it than that. I couldn't stop thinking about old Mr. Westcott and all the children at the children's hospital. As much as I tried to avoid it, I kept thinking about Mom and wondering how she was doing. At least she had Lyle to take care of her. I kept trying to bury thoughts of Mom, so I wouldn't have to face my growing worry and loneliness for her.

One night I had a particularly vivid nightmare that made me wake up panting in fear. I was outside somewhere in a field, on a beautiful summer day. As I looked up at the sky, I noticed that the sun seemed to be getting bigger and bigger, closer and closer. I don't know how, but I was able to look directly at the sun, as it loomed closer toward me. As it neared, I could see bright storms raging on its surface and occasionally it would spit flares out the side. It grew hotter and I began to sweat, then my skin felt like it was burning. When it got so big and close that I could almost reach out to touch it, the grass around me started catching on fire. I could hear my dad yelling at me to run, but I couldn't move my feet.

Suddenly, there was an explosion and I woke up, panting and sweating. I wasn't sure if it was a real-life explosion that had woken me up or if I had just dreamed it, but a few seconds later a second explosion rocked our building. I jumped out of bed and ran to the living room where Dad was looking out the window toward the west. A huge fire raged across town, probably five or ten miles away, and the light from it lit up the entire western sky. All night long the fire burned, first gaining in area, then finally burning down by late morning. The oddest thing about the whole night was the absence of sirens. It was strange that in the past year that I'd lived downtown, I'd gotten so used to sleeping through sirens, but now I found the absence of them oddly unnerving. I never did go back to sleep, but just laid there thinking about the nightmare and the real fire just a few miles away.

By December—at least according to one of our neighbors who kept track of the days religiously—almost everyone was out of their stockpile of food and the stores were empty, too. The military could only bring in water trucks every other day and rioting around them became more common and more intense. Dad and I started collecting rainwater in buckets on our little balcony, but it wasn't nearly enough to quench our thirst, let alone to use it for bathing and flushing the toilet. People began having to go to the bathroom outside, in parks and alleys. They were collecting rainwater that had pooled in the city's two hundred fountains, but the water in those were fouled from animals who were starving and dying from thirst, sometimes in the fountains themselves, and people who bathed in them. Kansas City used to be famous for its beautiful fountains, but now those same fountains were making people sick with dysentery and other awful stomach diseases that I'd never even heard of before. I got used to being hungry, but I couldn't get over the thirst that choked me and made me feel weaker every day.

At some point, the military began bringing in grain from grain elevators that had been taken over under martial law and handing it out to people with the water rations. Anyone who rioted was not allowed any water or grain and if the situation got too out of hand, the truck would simply leave that neighborhood and go somewhere else, so people started being more peaceful during the handouts. I think we all were getting too weak to fight anyway. The grain that was handed out was whole, hard, and straight from the field—not ground up or refined in any way. In order to eat it and digest it, you had to grind it and, especially in the case of soybeans, cook it. We mostly got corn, so to grind it, Dad broke one of his old bowling trophies off its marble base, and we used a piece of a broken concrete sidewalk to crack and grind the kernels against the marble. Then we'd mix a few drops of water with it, just so we could choke it down.

One day Dad and I noticed a pigeon hopping around on our balcony and we started thinking about how great it'd be to have some meat to eat. All that afternoon we worked on making a trap out of a box, a stick, and some string, just like Wile E. Coyote would do. When we finally got it perfected, we set it out on the balcony with a few precious grains of corn inside and waited for the pigeon to come back. And waited. And waited. And waited some more. Finally, two days later, we came home from getting our water and grain ration to find the trap had been sprung and a pigeon was inside. We cheered and did a little victory dance, but then reality set in and we realized we had no idea what to do with it now. Dad finally killed it with a knife and we spent the next hour trying to pluck feathers out of it. Then Dad stuck a serving fork in it and held it over an oil lamp we had made out of some cooking oil in a jar with string for a wick, until it was cooked. We devoured that thing and it seemed like the most delicious thing I'd ever eaten. We were still hungry afterward, but we felt more hope and more in control of the situation than we'd had in a long time and we set up more traps on the balcony and the roof of our building.

For the rest of that year, we lived off whatever animal we could trap, including mice and rats, and the water we collected off our balcony. People who only relied on the military rations didn't fare so well and many died from dehydration and starvation. Lots of people died from diseases, too, so Dad and I stayed in our apartment most of the time to avoid getting exposed to them, but we couldn't stay away from people completely.

Christmas came and went without much fanfare. Some people got together and prayed, but most people were too weak and depressed to feel like rejoicing. For the first time in my life, I couldn't care less that I didn't get any presents; I was just thankful to be alive, with a home, a little bit of food and water, and my Dad to take care of me.

Chapter 5
Fire and Loss

Just as I was beginning to think that Dad and I were going to pull through this crisis, Time decided to rear its spiteful face to play a horrible trick on me. In January it became bitterly cold, and without heat in the apartment, we were miserable, along with everyone else in the city. Try as we might to avoid catching any diseases, Dad and I came down with the flu. While mine just made me tired and achy, Dad's became much worse, with fever, chills and raspy breathing. I wondered if the possible broken ribs from the riot at the water tanker weeks before might have allowed pneumonia to settle in his lungs. I did what I could to help ease his pain. Dad didn't want me going alone to get our water and grain ration, so we tried to get by without it. But by the end of the week, Dad was becoming so dehydrated, I knew I had to go. I slipped out of the apartment while he was asleep.

I knew that Dad hadn't been eating as much as me—he would always take a few bites then say he was full and push the rest toward me—but I was shocked with how much weight he had lost in the last month. Since it had been so cold, we'd been wearing several layers of clothes to keep warm. It wasn't until Dad pulled off his layers of sweatshirts in one of his feverish fits, that I saw that he had been reduced to skin and bones, almost literally. I wanted to take him to the hospital, but after what he had seen there when he took old Mr. Westcott, he begged me to promise that I wouldn't take him.

— *They have nothing to help me there, son. No medicine, no sanitation, no power. The hospitals have become morgues. I'll be okay; I just need some sleep. I'm so tired...*

I promised, but I vowed to go back on it if he got much worse. At least I could go and try to find a doctor to come help him.

The day I left him alone at home to get our water and grain ration from the military truck, it was colder and grayer than ever, with the wind howling around every corner of the buildings downtown. Flurries started to fall and quickly developed into sleet. I thought about turning back and just letting my bucket fill with snow, which I could melt for water over our homemade oil lamp, but after seeing how thin Dad had become, I decided that he needed the grain to survive. So I stood, along with about a hundred other starving, freezing people in line for two or three hours. When I was nearing the front of the line, I started smelling smoke. At first, it was a pleasant smell, bringing back memories of roasting marshmallows around the little metal fire pit in our backyard at home when I was a kid. Even as I tried to push those treasured memories back down inside, the smell of the fire became stronger and more acrid. Because I was between tall buildings, I couldn't see where it was coming from, but the smoke was now curling around the buildings on both sides of me. I decided to stay to get the rations since I was so close to getting it, but after I got it, I hurried back toward our apartment.

About three blocks away, I couldn't even see anything anymore, the smoke was so thick. It was choking me and panic was quickly rising in my chest—not just because I couldn't breathe, but because I knew Dad was lying helpless back there in one of those buildings. It was almost certain that even if our building weren't the one on fire now, it would be by the time it was all over. I dropped my rations and ran around the buildings the other way, trying to come from the opposite direction so I could get into our building to get Dad out. People were swarming from the direction of the fire, covered in black soot, choking and coughing. I tried to stop some of the people I recognized from my building, asking them if they'd seen Dad, but they just shook their heads and struggled on.

I could only get within two blocks of the building before the smoke overcame me. I'm not sure whom, but someone dragged me out by my arm into the clear air and then ran on without a word. I was crying by then; I didn't care who saw me. When I finally caught my breath, I tried to beg bystanders to help me go in to get dad, but they all said it was impossible. I'd never felt so helpless and furious in my life. Just because I had left Dad to get the food and water he needed to survive, just at that precise moment in time, just in the amount of time I stood in that line—all those things Time used against me to take away the most important person in my life. I cried and yelled but my voice was only one of the many, crying out over the loss of home, worldly goods, and loved ones.

At one point, I found Officer Ortiz helping an older woman who was sitting on the curb get to her feet so she could move on to safety. I pestered him about going in to try to save my dad until he just came out and told me the unavoidable, crushing truth.

— *Kid, I'm sorry. If he got out you might find him wandering around, but if he's not out by now, he ain't comin' out.*

Officer Ortiz looked at me with sadness and pity in his eyes. He started to say something else, then changed his mind and told me I'd better find someplace to spend the night because it looked like this snowstorm was going to get worse. I spent the rest of the afternoon there anyway, looking through the throngs of people for Dad. Mobs of people were standing as close to the fire as they could without being choked by the smoke, because at least it was warm. We kept having to move back as the fire spread from building to building, devouring whole blocks as it went. It was incredible that it could still be burning so ferociously with all the snow that was falling.

As I was standing there, I couldn't help thinking about the nightmare I had had about the sun burning my skin and wondered if that was how it had been for Dad. Even though a tiny place in me still held out hope that he got out somehow, I knew he wasn't strong enough to even yell at anyone to come help him, let alone get out of bed. I couldn't get the image of Dad's skin on fire out of my head and that spurred me to keep looking for him.

When darkness began to fall and it was too dark to clearly see the faces of the people around me, I dazedly followed some people I had been standing next to as they wandered away from downtown. I was numb by that time, numb with cold and numb with emptiness. Somehow we wound up at the old Union Station building and found a place that had been broken into, where hundreds of people were setting up for the night. It was apparent that some of the people had been there for a while, but most of them were newcomers displaced by the fire. Everyone was exhausted, cold, hungry, and depressed. Desperation showed in their eyes, even though we were all too tired to do anything about it. There were a few children among us, though not as many as I would have thought—a depressing thought in itself—and they were crying quietly or just staring listlessly with big, round eyes. It was as if the life inside of all of us had died in that fire.

I slept fitfully that night on the cold marble floor, and kept waking up with a start to the sound of people screaming or crying out in their sleep. Other times I'd dream I was suffocating and I'd wake up crying, agonized about the thought of Dad gasping for air. Even though the pain of my loss was unimaginably immense, I knew that everyone else was feeling the same way, and that was oddly comforting.

In the morning, the snow had finally stopped blowing and some of us trekked through the shin-deep snow back downtown. From quite a distance, we could see huge plumes of billowing smoke, but no flames. We could also see two of the tallest buildings, one of which was where Dad used to work, were still standing, although covered in black soot almost to the top. When we got closer, we could see that many of the buildings that made up downtown had been burned, some to the ground. Those that were left had heavy smoke damage and some were still smoldering. It reminded me of the pictures I'd seen of Hiroshima after it was nuked in World War II.

A nice woman next to me asked me what I planned to do now, and I just looked at her vacantly for a minute. I knew that I had to move on, to figure out some kind of plan, but I couldn't make my mind work just yet.

— *Don't you have any family or friends you can go to?*

It took me several more seconds to think of Mom; I'm not sure why. I think my mind was just numb and I didn't want to associate the horror of what I had gone through with her. I think I was also a little scared that if I thought about her, I might lose her, too, so I shook my head at the lady. She smiled and gently took my hand.

— *You come with me then. I have a brother that lives just across the river. I'm sure he'd let you stay for a while until you find someplace.*

The lady tried to talk to me at first, told me her name was Lydia, but I just walked on in silence. I think she probably realized that I was in shock, or maybe she thought I was mute, but in either case, she quit trying and we just walked on through the dirty, soot-covered snow.

43

I followed the lady, making a wide arc around the burned out section of downtown and across one of the bridges over the Missouri river. I remember looking down at that river as we crossed, noticing how peacefully it was flowing, even with the thick blanket of snow covering its banks, and thinking that it had no clue about the suffering that was happening all across the land that it flowed through. I kept thinking that if I could just float down that river, eventually I'd find a warm place that was unaffected by all this despair. It was so tempting to just let myself fall in and be taken by the river, but something stirred inside me—life, I guess—and I kept on following the lady, who didn't even know my name.

Chapter 6
Water and Warmth

When we were nearing Lydia's brother's house, I started smelling burning wood, but it didn't register in my thick, clouded mind until I saw several thin, wispy columns of smoke rising in the distance. I stopped in my tracks and stared, fearing another huge inferno ahead. Lydia must have noticed the fear in my eyes, because she stopped and said gently,

— *It's okay; most of the homes in this neighborhood have fireplaces.*

It took a few seconds for that to sink in, but when it did, I started walking again with increased urgency to get there. It was late afternoon now and bitterly cold. I couldn't feel my feet or my face, and I knew that Lydia must have been freezing, too. As terrified as I now was of fire, the thought of a chance to get warm overwhelmed my fear, and now I couldn't wait to get there.

The neighborhood was quiet and clean, unlike downtown. In the twilight it looked like it was out of a fairytale, untouched by the events of the last few months. It was only as we got closer that I noticed the many tree stumps in the yards—ornamental trees that had been cut down for fuel. The few trees that were left in the yards and a nearby park were huge old-growth trees, whose lower branches had all been hacked off, their ragged stumps protruding from the trunk like amputations gone wrong. Nevertheless, the neighborhood seemed magical to me and in my overtired, overwrought, starved and dehydrated brain I started to believe that I might be in heaven.

When we got to the house, Lydia's brother was ecstatic to see her. It was obvious that he hadn't heard from her for a while and feared for her safety when downtown was burning. He looked at me a little warily, but invited me in anyway, apparently trusting his sister's instincts. Lydia introduced her brother as Roger, his wife as Silvia, and their daughter, who seemed to be about nine or ten years old, as Whitley. I was able to choke out my name through my cracked, frozen lips and parched throat. Roger led Lydia and me into the living room where the fireplace was sending out rays of wonderful heat, then handed us large cups of clear, warm water. I gulped it down, marveling that they had so much water to drink. After the cup was empty, he filled it again and I gulped it down, as well. After the third cup, Roger told me I should slow down or I would get sick. He said that since it had snowed, they had plenty of water that they could melt over the fireplace. They didn't have any food they could offer, though, and that was fine by me. I wasn't hungry anymore, now that my belly was full of water. I managed to squeak out a reply.

— *Thanks, I'm good now.*

After I warmed up a bit, I took a look around at the family. Lydia was talking softly with her brother and his wife, while their daughter was sitting on the floor across the room staring at me with her huge dark eyes. I noticed that like everyone else I'd seen lately, this family was skinny and their faces had a sickly, grayish tint surrounding eyes that appeared larger than normal and sunken into their heads. It reminded me of some of the people in anime movies, the really sad ones like *Grave of the Fireflies*. I knew then that I wasn't in heaven and that these people were suffering, too, although they seemed to have it a little better than the people in the downtown area had. At least they had some heat and now water to drink. The little girl motioned me over to her and I decided to go since I felt a little awkward just standing there by the fire.

Another thing I noticed, as I sat on the floor by Whitley, was the absence of much furniture. There was a sofa, on which was seated Roger and Lydia, and a recliner that Sylvia was sitting in. Other than that, there was not another chair, no end tables, bookcases, or any other piece of furniture that you'd expect to see in a house such as this. Lamps and a few knickknacks were placed on the floor near the walls and there was a big pile of blankets on the floor behind the sofa. Whitley tentatively began a conversation.

— *Your name's Ben, right?*

I nodded.

— *I'm Whitley.*

— *That's an unusual name. Where'd you get it?*

I knew my reply had sounded lame, but I couldn't think of anything else to say.

— *My mom's middle name is Whitney and my dad's middle name is Lee.*

When I still looked perplexed, she continued.

— *You know, Whit Lee.*

48

— Oh, I get it.

— Who are you named for?

— My dad named me after Benjamin Franklin, I guess. He admired him.

My voice cracked at the mention of my dad and I looked down quickly to hide the tears that threatened to spring to my eyes. While I was struggling to take control of my tingling eyes, I focused on my name and why I was named that. I know Dad was a fan of Benjamin Franklin, but I wasn't sure if it was the man he loved or the $100 bill that bore his portrait. As for my middle name, Matthew, I didn't know where that came from, but then out of the blue, I remembered that Mom's maiden name was Matthews and all of a sudden I had an immense yearning to see her again and to be held in her arms. I knew then that I had subconsciously been following Lydia because she was heading north, the direction of Mom's house. Somehow the thought of being halfway to Mom's cheered me and I was able to answer when Whitley asked me,

— How old are you?

— I'll be fifteen in April. How about you?

— I'm almost thirteen. In May.

49

That surprised me. I didn't think she was older than ten, but I realized it was probably because of her emaciated condition. I probably looked a lot younger than I was, as well. She sounded sad when she spoke next.

— *I don't think my dad will let you stay. We don't have enough food for us as it is, and now with Aunt Lydia...*

She shook her head apologetically.

— *That's ok. I'm headed to my mom's house up north.*

I smiled to show her that I understood her family's predicament.

— *You want to know what I miss most?*

She sounded wistful and young. I figured she was going to say that she missed going to school, seeing friends, texting on her cell phone, or something like that, but she surprised me again.

— *I miss reading before I go to sleep. I always used to read until I couldn't keep my eyes open anymore. Now it's too dark and I just lie there in the dark, not able to go to sleep.*

— *Don't you have any candles that you could read by?*

— *Oh, no. Those we burned in the first month. And the flashlight batteries gave out the first week.*

— I can show you how to make a lamp out of cooking oil if you have some.

Whitley's eyes grew bright even in the dim light of the fireplace.

— I think we have some in the pantry! Let's go see.

Whitley jumped up and grabbed a small piece of wood stacked on the floor beside the fireplace. It appeared to be the leg off some piece of furniture and it dawned on me why the house was so empty. They were forced to burn pieces of their wood furniture to keep warm. Whitley held the end of the piece of wood in the fire until it lit, then led me through the kitchen to the pantry. The fire from the stick was dim but we could see the few items left on the pantry shelves, mostly non-food items like trash bags and dishwashing liquid. There was no cooking oil, however, there was a big can of Crisco. She held it out to me.

— Will this work?

— I don't know why we couldn't try it and see.

It took Whitley a little time to talk her dad into letting us use it. He thought they might have to eat it to stay alive, but finally decided that if they were reduced to eating shortening, they wouldn't live long after that anyway, so he let her have it. She gave him a big hug with tears in her eyes and I could tell that he was happy to see her smile for once. We found some string and a small stick, which I used to poke a hole down the middle of the shortening. Then I pushed one end of the string down into it, leaving about a half an inch sticking out the top. Whitley used the lit piece of wood to light the end of the wick. It flickered at first, then began to burn brightly after the shortening around it melted a little. It was amazing how much light it put off and soon the rest of the family was gathered around it, marveling at my ingenuity.

Later that night, Whitley happily read herself to sleep wrapped in blankets on the floor behind the sofa with the Crisco lamp burning brightly. While Lydia slept on the sofa, I was ecstatic to be able to sleep in front of the fireplace, my yearning for warmth winning out over my fear of fire. Sylvia smiled at me gratefully as she blew out the wick on her way to bed.

In the morning, Roger showed me the traps that he and his neighbors had devised for trapping small animals, like squirrels and rabbits, in the neighborhood. He told me that at first they were successful, but now there weren't many animals left in the neighborhood. He said that he now spent a good portion of each day walking the three miles or so down to the banks of the Missouri River to set traps for birds, rats, squirrels, or any other animal he was lucky enough to catch. He had to stay to guard them, though, or someone else would steal the trapped animal and often the trap itself. Most days he came home empty handed, but sometimes he would get lucky and catch two or three animals.

Roger reluctantly told me I could stay with them, as long as I caught my own food. He made it clear that although they were willing to share their house, there wasn't enough food to go around and I could tell it was hard for him to say it, both because he didn't want to feel obligated to share and because he felt bad about turning a needy kid away. I didn't mind, though. I knew they had to take care of family first and they had absolutely no reason to open their home to me, a stranger. I assured him that I wouldn't be staying much longer. As soon as the weather warmed up a little I was going to head out for my mom's house up north.

Chapter 7
Homecoming

I stayed a week with Whitley and her family. I didn't eat much, but at least I was warm and had water to drink. I liked the family and they were pretty nice to me, especially when I bagged a couple of rabbits in a park down by the river and gave it to them for letting me stay, but I began thinking about Mom all the time. I found I didn't care anymore about the divorce and remarriage—I just wanted her to hold me in her arms again. I left one morning when the sun was shining and I had hope in my heart. Roger told me before I left that if things got bad, I could come back and stay with them. I couldn't imagine a reason that I would do that.

It had snowed twice more since the day of the fire, but it had melted some, too, so the highway I was following was sloshy and uncomfortable. I walked from early morning until after dark, but arrived at Mom's before it was very late. I was so happy to see the house, the same house I had spent so much time avoiding the past two years, time that could have been spent with Mom. I felt the lost Time like a finger poking my heart and vowed to make up for it now.

I knocked on the door—the doorbell didn't work without electricity, of course— and after several minutes, Lyle answered the door. At least I thought it was Lyle; I barely recognized him at first and I was shocked by his appearance. He was thin and unshaven; his clothes were stained and torn. A long way from the handsome, self-assured doctor he had been last time I'd seen him. He stared at me for a few seconds before he recognized me, then he smiled sadly and invited me in.

He led me into the living room, where he had a fire burning in the fireplace and asked me if I wanted something to drink. I nodded and he gave me a cup of water, apologizing that he didn't have any pop or anything else to offer me. He seemed odd, but I just figured it was the situation we were all in.

— *Where's Mom?*
— *She's not here...*

Lyle looked away and wrung his hands together like he was trying to hold on to something, but not succeeding.

— *Your mother…*

He looked at me then and his eyes teared up. It was a few seconds before he could go on, but I didn't want him to. I wanted to shout, *NO! Don't tell me!*, but I just stood there dumbfounded, while the finger poking my heart turned into a fist.

— *I'm sorry, Ben. She passed away three days ago.*

The fist suddenly slammed into my heart and I felt my whole body crumpling under the blow. Lyle caught me before I hit the floor, then he held me in his arms like I was a little kid and cried into my neck. I couldn't cry, I couldn't breathe, I couldn't see, I couldn't hear. I felt like I had died, like the blow was too great and that my heart had stopped beating right then and there. I don't know how long Lyle held me, but after a while he gently laid me on the sofa by the fire and covered me with a very soft, warm blanket and left the room. I remember lying there thinking, *This must be it, this must be heaven. It's warm and soft; I'm not hungry or thirsty. The only thing missing is Mom and Dad.* Then I got mad. I finally started crying hot, angry tears. It was my old enemy Time again—three days, I missed her by three days. If I had left Whitley's house the day after I'd arrived, I could have seen her, saved her. I could have at least apologized for turning my back on Time before the CME, time we could have spent together, time I could have forgiven her, told her I loved her, and time we could have used to make new happy memories. Now there was no time; there would never be time again. I felt the crush of guilt for blaming Time and Mom, instead of myself.

I think I lay on that couch, drifting in and out of consciousness for a few days; I no longer cared how many days were passing. Lyle brought me water, spooned some kind of weak broth into my mouth, and every so often, something bitter tasting dissolved in water. I hoped it was poison, but I think it was probably some kind of medicine. He also put cold compresses on my forehead when I was feverish and tucked extra blankets around me when I shivered. I dreamed about Dad and fire, and Mom and snow, sometimes even when I was awake. I thought if I lived, I would be insane. I deserved worse.

After a number of days, I awoke one morning with a clear head. The sun was shining through the big bay window in the living room and I smelled something cooking. It smelled delicious and for the first time in months, I was hungry. I tried to sit up, but got dizzy and had to lie back down until the spell passed. I tried again, slower this time, and was able to stay upright. Lyle came in then and smiled his sad smile.

— *Glad to see you back among the living.*

I wasn't glad to be back, but I just nodded my head.

— *I stitched up a little girl's arm last night and gave her some antibiotics to keep it from getting infected. Her father insisted that I take some food in payment. Of course, I refused at first—God knows no one has food to spare—but they're Mormons and they have those food storage caches. Anyway, I finally let him give me some cans of soup and he even threw in some crackers.*

Lyle was talking as he checked my temperature and looked into my eyes and throat with a little penlight. I was amazed that the battery still worked; I hadn't seen a flashlight in months, but I guess he probably just used it for short periods of time to check patients. After he seemed satisfied that I was going to live, he went to the kitchen and brought back a steaming cup of soup on a plate, surrounded by crackers. I remembered that this house had four fireplaces, one of which was in the kitchen. It had seemed so ostentatious the last time I was here, but now I felt bad for judging Lyle so harshly.

After I had eaten, I slept for most of the day, as it was dark again when I woke up to the sound of the front door being closed. Lyle came in to check on me while taking off his coat, hat, and gloves and warming his hands over the fire. He gave me another of his now familiar sad smiles and turned back to staring at the fire, saying nothing. I sat up slowly, cleared my throat, reached for the cup of water that Lyle had left on the coffee table, and struggled to make a sound come out of my raspy throat.

— *Another patient?*

— *Yes... Not as good an outcome this time, I'm afraid.*

He pressed his lips together and closed his eyes. I decided I didn't want to know exactly what that meant, so I said nothing. After several minutes, Lyle finally turned to me and said,

— Are you hungry? I can make another can of soup for you.

— That would be really nice, thank you.

Lyle returned later with two mugs of soup and we ate in silence. After we were done, Lyle took the dishes into the kitchen and returned some time later with something in his hand. He gave it to me, then sat down on the sofa opposite mine, watching me as I looked at the object in my hand. It was the watch pin I had given Mom over two years ago. It was stopped at 11:47 a.m. and the little date at the bottom said Nov 1. I just stared at it until Lyle said,

— The last thing she told me was "Give this to Ben; tell him I love him more than Time itself."

A tear rolled down my cheek and fell onto the face of the watch, then many more began to fall. Lyle handed me a hand towel to wipe my face. After a while, I asked,

— How... why'd she die?

— Your mom had been helping me go door-to-door to take care of sick people. She would normally wear a mask when there was some kind of communicable disease, but one little girl who had the flu or pneumonia was scared of the mask, so your mom took it off to soothe her and care for her. She

stayed with the family, caring for that sick little girl for four days until she recovered. Unfortunately, though, your mom couldn't recover from it after she came down with it. I did all I could, but it just wasn't enough.

Lyle stared at me for a second, his eyes begging for forgiveness, then looked down, resignedly, at his hands folded in his lap. He seemed to be struggling with the fact that he could not save her.

— *Where is she now? I mean, where'd you bury her?*

— *Well, Ben, I haven't been able to bury her; the ground's been too frozen. I made her a box and she's in it... out in the shed out back.*

He seemed almost apologetic as I stared at him. The thought of putting my mother, my precious, beautiful mother, in a box in the shed seemed like an outrage, an assault on everything good and pure and reasonable.

— *I didn't know what else to do, Ben. You've got to understand, there's nowhere else I could take her. I tried to dig a grave for her, but I couldn't get deep enough. I'll finish it when the ground thaws a bit. You can help if you want to.*

— *No! Mom deserves better than that! You know she deserves better than a box in the shed!*

Lyle had tears in his eyes when he replied.

— *I know, I know, Ben. I didn't know what else to do. I didn't want to take her to the morgue and just throw her in with hundreds of other bodies. I want to bury her here, in our backyard, so I can go out and talk to her every day, so we can talk to her. Please understand...*

I stood shakily, weakly, and stuffed Mom's watch into my pocket. I grabbed my coat as I made my way to the back door, ignoring Lyle's pleas to lie back down and rest. I had to see Mom; I had to see that she was okay, that she was properly taken care of.

The cold air gave me a burst of adrenalin and I jogged across the huge acre lot to the back of the yard where the shed stood. The moon was nearly full and I was able to see quite clearly. I stopped in front of the shed door and took several deep breaths as I built up my courage to enter.

I went in, leaving the door open to add to the dim light coming through the two windows. The shed had been cleared of all the mundane lawn equipment that it used to house, instead having just one long, narrow box in the middle. Lyle had placed a few trinkets on top, which meant nothing to me, so I laid them aside and opened the top. I braced myself for the odor of death that I remembered Mr. Westcott having, but there was nothing but a slightly sweet perfume smell. Mom's body was wrapped in a quilt on top of which was a bouquet of dried flowers. I thought it was probably her wedding bouquet.

I gently pulled the quilt away from her face and then recoiled in shock. I had expected her to look almost the same as the last time I'd seen her, maybe a little thinner, but I didn't expect to see her skin look so white, so frozen. I remembered how much she hated being cold, and I couldn't stand it any longer. I covered her back up and quickly put the lid back on her coffin. I ran from the shed, choking on my sobs. I stood outside the back door crying for a long time until Lyle came out and gently forced me back in. I was too weak to put up much resistance. He just kept saying,

— *I'm sorry, Ben, I'm really sorry.*

Chapter 8
Haunting Beauty

I knew I couldn't stay there in that house much longer. Even though it was a much better place than I'd lived in a long time, I couldn't get over the fact that my mom was lying out there in the shed in the back yard, cold and alone. I had dreams of her coming into the house and trying to climb under the covers with me as I slept in order to get warm. Other times, I'd dream that I would wake up, hearing her voice, and find her sitting at the kitchen table talking to Lyle. But she wasn't normal; her skin looked gray and when she looked at me, her eyes looked dark and dead. I woke up screaming many times in the next few days.

Several days later, I felt strong enough to leave. I figured I'd tried to go back to Whitley's house even though I hated to be a burden to that family. Lyle tried to talk me into staying, but I just couldn't face another night in that house; it held too many ghosts for me. I felt sorry for Lyle. I just couldn't see him as the bad guy anymore after he'd been so good to me and all the other people he helped, medically, since I'd been there, and never once asked for any kind of payment in return. I could tell he was lonely and that he really wanted me to stay with him. I thought he probably saw a little of my mom in me and wanted to hold on to that connection to her. I found myself yearning for that too, but in the end, I just couldn't stand the ghosts.

The day I left was a much warmer day, although still quite blustery. I think it must have been getting closer to spring. While I was walking on the highway, a flashing light on one of the off-ramps startled me. I began to see more and more lights the further I walked toward the center of town: streetlights, lights in buildings and houses, lighted business signs. The power was back on! I looked around in amazement at the reawakening of civilization. People were out in the streets, cheering and hollering, hugging family and neighbors. By the time I reached Whitley's house, their power was back, too. Everyone was whooping and hollering inside the house. I could hear them even before I rang the doorbell. When it sounded, I could hear a squeal of delight and footsteps racing to open the door.

Whitley threw open the door and embraced me in a big hug. I was a little embarrassed by her enthusiasm, especially when I saw that there were two other girls standing beside her, all with big grins on their faces.

— *Mom, Dad, Aunt Lydia! Look who's here!*

Several people rushed into the front room while Whitley pulled me into the house. Roger, Silvia, and especially Lydia seemed very happy to see me, and I was warmed by such a heartfelt welcome. After many confused minutes with everyone talking all at once, asking me questions, exclaiming over the fact that the power was back on, etc., Whitley pulled me into her bedroom with the two girls and introduced them to me as her cousins. One was a younger girl named Mikayla and the other was a stunningly beautiful girl named Sara. I found out that they were not sisters, though, but cousins to each other, as well.

While Whitley and Mikayla were both pretty girls, in a malnourished sort of way, I just couldn't keep my eyes off Sara. She had shoulder length, smooth, blond hair that curled out at the ends like the petals of an opening rose. Her eyes were big, deep pools of the lightest blue, like pictures I'd seen of the Caribbean on flyers that Mom had brought home to try to get Dad to take her on vacation the year before the CME. She was small, not much bigger than her younger cousins, but then all of us were mere slivers of what we used to be by then. She had beautiful, full lips that curved ever so slightly up when the other girls giggled about something, but even while smiling she looked sad, and her eyes had a haunted quality about them. I could tell that the past few months had taken a toll on her, much more so than on her cousins.

After an hour or two of listening to girl chatter, during which Sara was mostly silent, like me, Sara asked me if I'd like to go for a walk outside. I was suddenly struck with fear of what I must smell like since I hadn't had a shower or a full bath in months. We had run out of deodorant and soap a long time ago, and the best we could do to keep somewhat clean was to rub snow and a handful of baking soda all over.

It was pretty dark by then, but I agreed to go for a walk with her because there was no way I could say no to that lovely girl, and the thought of being alone with her made my heart pound in my chest. I felt more alive around her than I had since before the CME. We grabbed our coats and walked around the neighborhood, which was now lit with just a few streetlamps, some having been damaged during the CME. Luckily, she started the conversation, as I felt quite tongue-tied around her.

— *How old are you?*

— *I'll be fifteen in April. Wait, is it April yet?*

— *No, it's still March.*

She looked at me quizzically, then said,

— *I turn sixteen in July. I can't wait until July!*

— *You're lucky.*

We walked in silence for a few seconds, then she spoke again, as if trying to find something to say to fill the empty space.

— *My name is Sara. But then you already knew that, didn't you?*

— *Yeah, it's a beautiful name, though.*

I looked down at my feet then said, barely above a whisper,

— *It was my mother's name.*

I don't think she heard the past tense in my words because she exclaimed,

— *Your mom's name is Sara? What a coincidence! Does she spell it with an "h" at the end? I don't.*

— *Yeah, she spelled it with an "h."*

I paused for an uncomfortable second, then said,

— *She died a few weeks ago. My dad, too.*

I looked away and squeezed my eyes shut to stop the tears that were prickling at the back of them. Her voice was quiet when she answered.

— *Oh, I'm sorry. My parents died last month. The flu.*

— *Yeah, mine, too.*

I didn't feel like explaining about the fire. I didn't really want to talk about them at all, but just knowing that Sara and I were both orphans made me feel suddenly close to her, like we belonged to some secret club that only orphans could be in. She must have felt the same because she reached out and took my hand in hers and we continued walking around the block like that until we got cold and headed back to the house.

— *Are you going to stay at Uncle Roger's?*

— I was hoping to, but it looks kind of crowded now. Maybe I should just find somewhere else.

— Do you have anywhere else to go?

— I don't know. I'll find something.

I shrugged and looked away.

— No, please stay, for a while at least. They're already talking about sending us back to school and I'm not going. So I may not be here for very long either. How about you? Do you want to go back? To school, I mean?

I'd never even thought about going back to school. After all I'd been through, after all everyone had been through, it just seemed absurd to do something as normal as going back to school. If I did, I knew I'd be forced into a foster home or maybe even an orphanage, and the thought of either one of those terrified me for some reason.

— No way. I'm not going either!

— Let's just run away together. There has to be tons of abandoned buildings or empty houses we could live in. We've survived without power for five months; we could survive alone until we're 17. After that, we could legally be on our own.

— How do you know that?

— Uncle Roger told me I have to stay with him until I could be legally emancipated at 17. But I'm not staying if he's going to force me to go to school! I just couldn't stand the drama and the pity.

I understood exactly what she was saying. I also didn't want to face seeing how many of my friends hadn't made it through the winter. It was much better to just believe that they were carrying on their lives like nothing had happened. But I knew my life was forever changed. And Sara's too. She made so much sense that I agreed immediately and we began to think of ways to make our escape.

Chapter 9

Sara

Sara and I grew close over the next few days. It was amazing how everyone around us was looking forward to life getting back to normal, while Sara and I knew it never would for us. Everything just seemed so superficial and unimportant now, like TV, school, and phones. The only thing we wanted to do was talk to each other, hold hands and, starting that first night I met her, when she gave me a quick peck on the lips, kissing each other. Our kisses were sad, though, like we were doing it just to share our sorrow with each other.

Landline phones were partially functional, although service to every household and most long distance service had not yet been restored. Cell phones were still out and would probably not be usable for quite some time since most of the satellites, which relay the calls, had been lost. We found that out from the news on TV, which was the only programming, besides reruns, that was available. The newscasters were calling the day of the CME "Power Failure Day", or PF Day. I didn't care to watch TV, though, I didn't feel like playing video games, and I didn't have anyone that I cared to call. I was afraid to try to call my grandparents in New York in case they had died, too. Better to just go on believing that they were fine.

The one electronic thing that Sara and I did enjoy together was listening to her iPod, which is the first thing she plugged in to charge when the power was back on. She had a great mix of songs in lots of different styles, from classical to country to rock and even a little rap. I was familiar with some of the songs, but there were many that I'd never heard before. Sara's favorite song, which we listened to together, one earphone in her ear and the other in mine, was *If I Die Young* by The Band Perry. She loved that song and would sing along with the iPod or even by herself when she wasn't listening to it. The words made me so sad, but she said they gave her hope. I don't know what hope she could find in them; all I heard was sadness. Her favorite line, she said, was the part about God making her a rainbow so she could shine down on her mother, but she said she thought of it the other way around, that her mother was the rainbow shining down on her. Another line she loved said to save her tears in her pocket for when she really needed them. She would pat her left jean pocket and say that it was full of tears. I didn't tell her, but I kept my own tears of a sort, stuffed down deep in my pocket: Mom's watch pin—even though it no longer kept time, it was a reminder of how much time I'd let slip away when I'd had a chance to use it wisely.

A song that I liked and would listen to over and over was *Mad World* by Gary Jules. It made me sad, too, but it seemed like I needed to be sad now, like if I heard a happy song it would cheapen all that I'd been through. The words of that song held so much meaning for me. I know when it was written the words were talking about people scurrying around in their busy lives, not pausing to consider what's important, but since the day of the CME and all the terrible things that had happened thereafter, the meaning of the words changed in ways I don't think the songwriter could have imagined. My chest would always feel kind of hollow when I heard the words about hiding my head and drowning my sorrow, because there's no tomorrow. That's how I felt: like my life, like Time, had stopped and there was no future for me, just today plodding on and on, going nowhere in this mad world.

Sara had a pocketful of cash from her parents, not in the pocket where she sym-bolically stashed her tears, but in her right front pocket of her jeans, where she claimed no one could pickpocket her. She took it out and showed it to me, a wad of $100 bills—Benjamins—and said we would use it to start a new life for ourselves. We began to collect things we'd need, like blankets, warm clothes, extra coats, and water bottles, and stuffed everything into two large gym bags. We got most of it from Sara's old house, which was just a few blocks away and still stood empty. She said we couldn't stay in it when we ran away, though, because that's the first place they'd look for us. School was set to start May 1st and we were supposed to register the week before. We decided to leave the night before my birthday, so we could celebrate our new life and my birthday together. I also wanted to be sure that the official date of our freedom wasn't the 13th, because I still didn't trust that number, but I didn't tell Sara about it. I just wasn't ready to open up yet about all my past problems. We had too many things to think about right then to dredge up old thoughts and memories.

We left shortly after midnight on April 12th, when we were sure the rest of the family was asleep. We had left our gym bags at Sara's old house, so we went there first. We were tempted to stay the night there, but we knew it was too risky, so we set out right away toward downtown. We had dressed in some of Sara's parents' clothes so that we would look older to people on the street. I had on one of her dad's suit jackets over my winter coat and one of those furry Russian hats on my head. Sara wore her mom's red wool pea coat, which looked much more mature than her pink parka.

We had to stay off the main highway this time, as there were a few cars back on the roads now, even though gasoline cost a fortune since the refineries had been slow to start back up after the power was back. We followed the general route of the highway, though, and when we came to the river we had to use the highway bridge to cross. It was early in the morning and no cars passed us as we crossed. This time, I was afraid to look down into the river, remembering what

I had felt the last time I'd crossed it so, instead, I just walked with my eyes focused on my feet. We were quiet most of the way; Sara only asked a few questions about where we were going.

Just before dawn we made it to the burned out section of downtown. We stopped and stared at it for several minutes, Sara in awe of the destruction, and me reliving the horror of that fateful day. As the sun rose and its rays peeked around the buildings to the east of us, it cast a pinkish-orange glow in strips amongst the dark shadows of burned-out buildings. It reminded me of the first few nights after PF Day, when the aurora borealis made strange reflections on the dark buildings at night, although those buildings were now mere rubble for the most part. I could only watch it for a few minutes before I turned away. Sara noticed my distress and grabbed my hand, saying,

— *C'mon. Let's find a place to stay.*

We headed toward a building at the edge of the destruction, one that had some fire damage on one side, but which was still mostly standing. We tried the front door of the building, but it was locked, so we went around back into the alley, looking for a back door. We found it. It looked like someone had tried to bash in the glass, as it was cracked like a spider web, but had not succeeded. They had been able, however, to break the lock and it hung off the frame, which had also been mangled. We entered cautiously. It was still quite dark, especially inside the hallway, and we had no idea what might be lurking inside. We made our way down the hallway, keeping our voices to a whisper, and quietly checking apartment doors to see if there were any that were unlocked. All on the first floor were locked, so we climbed the stairway at the end of the hall to the second floor and tried those doors, as well. It wasn't until we got to the third floor that we found an unlocked door.

This door opened into a room that faced south toward the destroyed part of downtown. As soon as we opened the door, we knew that we could not stay in that room. Part of the outer wall had been burned and was crumbling away. A cold wind blew in the hole and several birds were perched on the edge singing to greet the morning sun. We closed the door quickly and turned our attention to the north side apartments instead. At the end of the hall, we found one unlocked and we entered it cautiously.

The room looked like nothing had happened to the building, although the faint smell of smoke still hung in the air. We moved around quietly, checking each room to see if anyone was there. After finding it completely empty, I locked the front door and began to explore more carefully. The apartment contained the typical furniture: sofa, easy chair, coffee table, and television stand in the living room, but with no TV— that must have been taken by the previous owner or looted; little kitchenette at the end of the living room with a breakfast bar and three stools, but no table; bed, dresser, and bedside table with no lamp in the single bedroom. There were a few pieces of clothing still hanging amongst the many empty wire hangers in the closet, but no food in the kitchenette.

The bedding on the bed smelled strongly of smoke, so Sara stripped it off and pulled a blanket from her duffle bag. She smoothed it out on the bed and threw herself on top of it, exhausted. I pulled another blanket out and covered her with it, as she murmured thanks. I made myself a cozy bed on the sofa with yet another blanket, which we had brought with us. I was asleep almost as soon as my head hit the cushions.

Chapter 10
Getting Acquainted

I awoke later in the day just as the setting sun shined through the west-facing living room windows of the apartment. Sara was already up, washing her face in the cold tap water that was, surprisingly, flowing through the building's pipes. It had been so nice to have running water again after the power came back on at Whitley's house, but I didn't expect the water to be on in this partially burned out and abandoned building. Sara informed me that there was no hot water, though, so the excitement I'd felt at the thought of being able to take a hot shower quickly faded away.

We decided to leave the apartment to go and explore. We didn't have a key to lock it once we left, so we packed up our belongings and took our gym bags with us. As we walked down the three flights of stairs to the lobby, we could hear people talking and laughing and we were a little apprehensive about revealing ourselves, not knowing if we would be in trouble for trespassing or not. At the bottom of the stairwell, we paused and tried to listen for clues as to whether we would be welcomed or kicked out, or maybe even arrested for being there. Most of the voices sounded young, our age or a little older, but there was at least one voice that sounded like an older adult. We heard one boy saying that he thought some newcomers had occupied Apartment 326 and we were somewhat startled when we realized that that was the apartment we had stayed in earlier in the day. He didn't sound angry or conspiratorial about it; he sounded like he was just stating a fact. We drew in a deep breath, grabbed hands, and came out of our hiding place to face a crowd of about a dozen people standing around or sitting in the lobby.

Everyone looked our way immediately, some with suspicion in their eyes, but most with welcoming smiles. Sara bravely spoke for us.

— *Hi. I'm Sara and this is Ben. We need a place to stay. Is it all right if we stay here?*

The older man, who appeared to be in his forties or fifties, with a scraggly black beard laced with gray hair matching the receding hair on his head, smiled and answered,

— *Yes, you can stay in any of the unoccupied rooms. As long as you follow a few rules.*

Sara and I exchanged glances then nodded as he recited the rules of the building.

— *Rule number one: it's first come, first served around here. Most of the time we sleep in the same room every night, but if someone gets there before you do, you have to find somewhere else to sleep. It's a good idea to lock your door once you're in for the night so no one surprises you. Rule two: no lights after dark. The electricity is on in this building, but we don't want anyone to find out and turn it off. Please use it judiciously. You can use it to warm some water or cook some food on the stove or in a microwave if your apartment is lucky enough to have one, but do not turn on the heat or air conditioning. That would be sure to bring attention to us. We're all trying to live under the radar here, so to speak. That brings us to rule number three: do not tell anyone about us. By that, I mean don't invite anyone else to live here or tell anyone in a position of authority about the building. You found us by your own devices and as long as you follow our simple rules, we will allow you to stay here, but we don't want the world to know about us. Rule four: respect each and every one of us here. Any fighting, stealing, or being otherwise objectionable will result in you being expelled. Do you understand? Do you agree to these rules?*

Sara and I nodded in agreement, then the older man stuck out his hand to shake ours and said,

— *Welcome to the building. My name is Gerald. I'm kind of the father figure around here.*

After that, everyone else came forward and introduced themselves. Besides Gerald, there were only two other adults: a crusty old man who looked ancient, whom Gerald called Skinner, and a forty-something woman named Janice. Skinner barely lifted his eyes to look at us when Gerald introduced him. When he went back to staring at the floor, Gerald said in a low voice,

— *He scored a bottle of booze somewhere last night—first he's had in quite a while. He's an alcoholic. It's a wonder he made it through the bad times.*

Gerald shook his head sadly as he patted Skinner on the shoulder. Janice was much more friendly than the old man, smiling and shaking our hands when we were introduced. She said she was kind of like the mother to all the young people who stayed in the building. I ventured a question.

— *Are you and Gerald married?*

— *Oh heavens, no! We're just friends. Gerald and I lived here before the fire. After the fire, they forced us to leave, but we had nowhere else to go, so we came back. We have keys to our apartments.*

The rest of the group consisted of young men, teen boys really. Sara was the only girl of the bunch and she was getting some pretty hungry stares. Of course, even in a room full of girls, she would have stood out, as beautiful as she was. I put my arm around her shoulders just to send the message that she was taken, even though she and I had never declared that we were together officially, not even to each other, let alone to others. I half expected her to shrug me off and give me an angry look, but she seemed to welcome the security.

One boy about my age, called Sonny, offered Sara a bag of dried peas and she took it gratefully. If I weren't so hungry, I'd have told him to shove it, because I think he only shared it with her to try to lure her away from me. I vowed to myself that I'd find some food for us the next morning. Since it was already almost dark, everyone started leaving to find rooms to sleep in. Sara and I went back up to Apartment 326. She searched through the kitchen cabinets until she found a pot with a lid, then filled it with water and poured the entire bag of peas in. Since there was no microwave in the apartment, she put it on the electric stove and turned the burner on low. We sat on the couch and talked while the peas simmered.

I hadn't told Sara much about my parents and neither had she about her parents. It wasn't that we didn't trust each other, but just that we hadn't been ready to talk about it yet. For some reason, that night Sara felt like talking about her past. It might have been because Gerald and Janice reminded her of her parents or that she finally felt somewhat safe with me in that apartment. For whatever reason, she just started talking.

— *My mom had blond hair like me. She used to be a cheerleader for the Chiefs, back before she had me, before she got married.*

So that explained her unusually good looks. Dad used to watch the Chiefs every Sunday during football season, but I hadn't been too interested until I started playing football myself. Sara continued,

— *Dad was a teacher. He was handsome, but he was always amazed that Mom could love him because she could've married somebody with a lot more money than him. They really loved each other.*

Sara stopped and stared down at her hands for a while. I knew she was thinking about her parents, so I just sat quietly and waited for her to continue. She drew in a slow, ragged breath and started talking again, quietly.

— *Mom died first. I thought Dad would cry and scream but he didn't; he just sat and stared, almost never moving, until I woke up one morning and found him dead, still staring.*

Sara started to tremble then and I couldn't help trembling a little myself. I put my arms around her gently, timidly, and she cried for just a few seconds. Then she straightened up abruptly and wiped her eyes, almost angrily.

— *They weren't supposed to die. They were supposed to stay and take care of me!*

Her sudden anger took me by surprise and I must have had a dismayed look on my face, because she softened immediately and took my hand.

— At least I have you now.

After that, we listened to her iPod for a while, then Sara got up and checked the peas. They weren't completely done yet, but we were so hungry, we decided they were good enough. I found a couple of bowls and spoons and Sara poured us each a big helping. Between us we ate the whole pound of peas, broth and all. I remember thinking as I devoured it, that we should probably save half of it for tomorrow, but I couldn't stop myself from refilling my bowl again and again. Apparently, neither could Sara.

After we finished eating, Sara asked me about my parents. I felt I owed her some sort of explanation since she had opened up to me about her parents and she had shared the food that was given expressly to her. I felt a huge lump in my throat and my heart constricted as I slowly pried open the chest of memories in my brain to let out a few to share with Sara. When I spoke, I barely recognized my voice. It was low and raspy, like I had laryngitis or something.

— My mom left my dad and me a couple of years ago. She found somebody she liked better than us, I guess. My dad died alone in the big fire down here because I couldn't get to him in time. My mom died before I could

get to her, too. Time... my timing is never right.

Sara took my hands in hers and looked me in the eyes.

— *You know, things aren't always as they seem, Ben. Sometimes it seems one way when it's really another.*

I had no idea what she was talking about, so I just looked away and changed the subject, asking her what she thought we should do the next day. She let it drop and merely said,

— *I guess we've got to look for food.*

I nodded and Sara got up to go make her bed in the bedroom while I made mine on the sofa again.

Chapter 11

Foraging

The next morning I was awakened by a quiet knocking at the door. Sara was already up, quietly warming some water on the stove for a sponge bath, so she went to the door and looked through the peephole.

— *It's Sonny.*

I rolled my eyes and hurriedly shoved my blankets into my gym bag. I didn't want Sonny to see that Sara and I slept in separate beds. It was some macho thing, but I instinctively felt that she would be safer if everyone believed that we were really "together." Sara opened the door a crack with the safety chain still on, then after listening to Sonny's whispers for a second, leaned back in to me and said,

— *Sonny wants to talk to me for a sec. Be right back.*

I didn't want Sara to talk to him, especially in private, but what could I do? She stepped out into the hall and pulled the door gently closed behind her. I tried to listen to what they were saying, leaning my head close to the door, but all I could hear was mumbling. They must have been talking very quietly. After a couple of minutes, Sara came back in alone, as I hurried to busy myself with plumping up the pillows on the sofa. She didn't say anything for quite a while, but just went back to watching the pot of water warming on the stove. After about five minutes I couldn't stand it anymore and asked, trying to sound nonchalant,

— *So... what did Sonny Boy want?*

— *Please don't call him that. His name is Jason. They just call him Sonny because there's another Jason in the building.*

— *Why do you care so much all of a sudden?*

I hadn't meant to sound angry, but I couldn't help the jealousy from creeping into my voice. Sara gave me a disgusted look, but said nothing. I tried again, this time concentrating hard to make my voice sound neutral.

— *Okay, sorry. What did Jason want?*

He wants to take me to a secret food cache he's found.

— *You're not going, are you?*

— *Maybe. He said there's enough food there to feed us for several months.*

— But we were going to the river today to catch some fish or birds or something.

— You can still go there. Then we'll have plenty to eat.

— I don't want you to go with him.

— Why in the world not? Why wouldn't you want us to know where this is?

— Okay, then I'll go with you.

— No... He said only I could go.

— Oh, yeah, sure. That's convenient, isn't it?

— Why are you being such an ass? It's just that he doesn't trust guys. The other guys have been really mean to him.

Sara's voice rose in anger and frustration. I had a bad feeling about this, but I wasn't sure if it was because I sensed danger or just because I was jealous. I felt helpless. I felt that if I pushed it too hard, Sara would just leave me, but I still didn't want her to go with Jason. I could provide for her; I knew I could. We didn't need some punk coming in to try to prove to Sara that I couldn't. After an excruciating mental battle with myself, during which Sara stared at me angrily, I shrugged and gave up.

— Do whatever you want. I'm going to get us some fresh meat.

I put emphasis on "fresh meat," hoping

that it would somehow impress her more than canned or dried food. When she answered, her voice was softer, gentler, as if she finally understood the anguish I was feeling.

— *Good. I'd like that. I promise it'll be okay.*

With that, she put her hand on my cheek and kissed me tenderly and lightly on my lips. Then she smiled her beautiful, reassuring smile, although it didn't quite reach her eyes.

Sara cleaned herself up and gave me a quick peck on the cheek before leaving to meet up with Jason. She looked into my eyes, so deeply that I felt like I was swimming in her Caribbean blue eyes, and said softly,

— *Good luck. Be careful. I'll see you back here this afternoon.*

Part of me wanted to follow her and Jason, staying well hidden like a spy or a CIA agent. But another part of me wanted desperately to show her that I could provide for her by bringing home some fresh food. I finally decided to do that, even though my heart was squeezing in my chest as I left the apartment with my gym bag. First, I stopped by Janice's apartment and left Sara's bag and most of the contents of mine, as Janice had told us we could do as long as we shared some of the food we found while we were out foraging. That put more pressure on me than ever to find food, but I couldn't very well hunt with two large bags suspended from my shoulders and I didn't dare trust the others enough to leave them in our apartment.

It took me only half an hour to walk down to the river as the apartment building was fairly close to it. It was a pretty nice day and there were lots of people on the banks of the river already, foraging for food, many with fishing poles. Even though the electricity had been on for about a month, there still was not a lot of food to be had as manufacturers and grocery stores geared back into business. And even when they did, there was not a lot of food that had been grown commercially to be processed, since the shortage of gasoline kept large-scale farming to a minimum.

I had brought with me a telescoping fishing pole that had belonged to Sara's dad. I found a relatively empty spot on the river and dug around in the dirt for some worms. I wasn't very good at fishing, since my dad had never had time to take me, but I had once gone with my Cub Scout troop when I was six or seven. Mom had come along with me and helped me put the worm on the hook. As I struggled with it now, I suddenly remembered how she had grimaced then smiled at me and forced the worm onto the hook. I decided that was a memory I needed to keep, so I tucked it away in the back of my mind.

At first I was unsuccessful, but every time I thought about quitting, the image of Jason handing that bag of peas to Sara came into my mind and I renewed my determination to catch something. I think I had been there most of the day—Time was not something I cared to think about anymore, even though we now had clocks to mark it again—before I finally had some luck and was able to catch two small fish, which if I remembered correctly were called blue gill, and two larger fish, which could have been bass or trout or catfish, for all I knew. I gutted them, as I observed a fisherman down the way from me doing, stuck them in my bag, and headed for home as the sun was heading down in the west. I hurried, worried that Sara would be all alone in the apartment, or worse, that she'd be with Jason. I wanted to trust Sara, but I definitely did not trust him.

When I got back to the building, I stopped by Janice's apartment and picked up our stuff, leaving one of the small fish with her. She was thrilled to have fresh fish to eat and invited Sara and me to dinner, but I turned her down. I didn't feel much like sharing Sara with anyone else that day. Sara was already in the apartment when I got there, quickly unlocking the door when I knocked.

— I'm so glad you're home! I've been so worried about you. Did you get anything?

I smiled and, with a grand flourish, pulled out the remaining three fish. Sara squealed with delight and I felt better than I'd had all day. I was overwhelmed with relief and pride and just plain old love for that beautiful girl who was happily dancing around the living room with a dead fish for her partner.

Sara and I did the best we could to scale the fish and cook them, but we ended up having to pick some of the scales out of our teeth after eating. Neither of us knew much about cooking fresh fish, but they sure tasted good. Sara showed me the few items she had got from the food cache that Jason had taken her to: a bag of rice, four cans of vegetables, and two cans of peaches. We opened one of the cans of peaches for dessert. I wanted to ask her about her trip with him, but I didn't want her to know I was jealous and worried about it, so I just kept quiet.

After we ate, Sara pulled a Hostess cupcake twin pack out of her bag and told me happy birthday. I'd forgotten that it was my birthday. Most of the day had sucked, but I was touched that Sara had remembered me while she was with Jason. After we shared the cupcakes, we sat and talked for a while.

— *Tell me about when your mom left you, Ben.*

— *What do you want to know?*

— *I mean, did she just move out and leave you with your dad?*

— *Well... actually, Dad was the one who moved out.*

— *So did your mom make you go with him or something?*

— *No, I stayed with her for a few months, then I wanted to go live with my dad.*

— *So... then your mom didn't leave you; you and your dad left her. Right?*

I hadn't thought of it that way before. All of a sudden the truth hit me like a physical blow and I was confused, wondering if my memory was intact or if I had twisted the truth around in my mind to fit some made-up scenario. I was grasping for the reason I had blamed Mom for leaving us, but then I remembered Lyle.

— *Well, we had to leave. Mom had a new boyfriend.*

— *So why'd she have a boyfriend?*

— *How the hell am I supposed to know?*

I hadn't meant to raise my voice; I hadn't meant to bring up the old anger and heartache that the memory of my unlucky thirteenth year held for me, but I couldn't help it. I think part of me was trying to protect myself from trying to figure it all out, so I turned to anger to cover the raw feelings underneath. I was sorry the moment I looked at Sara's face, however. She seemed surprised, shocked maybe, with her eyebrows raised and trace of fear in her eyes. The happiness that I had seen in her eyes earlier in the evening, when she had twirled the fish around, was now replaced with the more familiar haunted look. I felt ashamed and looked away from her quickly, but she reached out and pulled my face back to look at hers.

— *I'm sorry, Ben.*

— No, I'm the one who's sorry. I didn't mean to yell at you. It's just that…

— I know. It's okay. I'm angry with my parents for leaving me, too. Even though it wasn't their fault. Just remember, things aren't always what they seem.

At that, she drew me into a hug and we sat for a long time in silence, before she got up and went into the bedroom for the night. I refused to think about what she had said or about why Dad and I had left Mom. It was still too painful and besides, I didn't see any use in reliving it. Better to let it all remain buried with my parents.

Chapter 12

Whatever It Takes

The next few days were spent trying to figure out ways to get food. Sara decided that as long as we had fresh food, she wouldn't go with Jason to the food cache. She reasoned that we couldn't store the canned food in the apartment since we were never sure we'd get the same one every night and we couldn't very well carry around more than a few cans with us in our bags everywhere we went. That was alright with me... well, more than alright. It meant less time Sara spent with Jason. I'd almost rather have starved than see her go with him again.

Since "our" apartment didn't have a balcony and we couldn't guarantee that we'd always get to stay in the same one anyway, Sara and I went up to the roof to set an animal trap kind of like the one Dad and I had set during the blackout. We had to be careful to stay away from the burned out portion of the roof because it didn't look too stable. We also stayed away from the other edges of the roof in case someone happened to look up and see us up there where we definitely weren't supposed to be. I found a piece of PVC pipe, about two feet in length and four inches wide, which I rigged as a trap. I had remembered reading somewhere that birds can't walk backwards, so I figured if I could lure them in, they'd be trapped. At least, that was what I'd hoped would happen. I covered one end of the pipe with some discarded wire mesh, then placed it in an out of the way spot on the roof, sprinkled some grains of rice leading to the pipe and down inside it, too.

While we were on the roof setting the trap, Sara found a wooden pallet, which gave her an idea for growing some of our own food. That night after dark, we went out to the strip of grass and trees that lined the street in front of the building and dug up fresh dirt with our hands and kitchen utensils. It was hard work but we managed to fill one of our gym bags with the dry dirt and drag it up to the roof. We packed the pallet with dirt between the slats. Now we just needed seeds. Sara said she'd seen some packets of vegetable seeds at the food cache that Jason had taken her to and planned to go there the next day with him. I wasn't too happy about that, but I saw the value in growing our own food; maybe then she would never have to go back there with him. Still, I was grumpy the rest of the evening thinking about her being with him. When we had finished and gone back to the apartment, which we were lucky enough to get again, Sara had had enough of my bad attitude and confronted me.

— *Ben, what's wrong with you tonight?*

— *Nothing.*

— *I know something's wrong.*

— *I don't know. I guess I just don't like the idea of you going with Jason tomorrow.*

— *What are you afraid of? That he'll rape me or something?*

— *Maybe. I don't trust him. I don't trust anyone.*

— *Well, he doesn't trust you either. Don't you trust me?*

I paused for just a second before I answered and that made Sara purse her lips in disgust. I tried to backpedal.

— *I trust you. I just don't know if...*

— *If what?*

She sounded angry now.

— *If he'll talk you into doing something you don't want to do. If he'll hurt you somehow.*

Then I lowered my eyes to the floor, miserably, and said, barely above a whisper,

— *If you'll decide you'd rather be with him than me.*

Sara lifted my chin up until I was looking into her eyes. Her voice was stern but not as angry.

— *That's not going to happen, Ben. I'm with you to the end. But I've gotta do whatever it takes to help us survive.*

Part of what she said made me happier, but a lot of it had me worried. The parts about *to the end*, and *whatever it takes* made me wonder what she meant. I wanted to ask her to explain, but decided to leave it until another time. I was never good at expressing my feelings out loud. Or even to myself for that matter. Sometimes it seemed easier just to bury them.

The next morning, Sara left with Jason as planned. She said that the food cache was quite a ways away and that they'd probably be gone until afternoon. She gave me a quick kiss before she left, but I didn't say anything. I didn't trust myself not to lash out again.

I knew I had to keep myself busy that day; my old enemy Time would come back to haunt me if I let it. So I decided to go down to the river and do some fishing again, but first, I checked the bird trap on the roof. No luck yet, but most of the rice had been eaten, so I added more to it. I stowed one bag and our extra gear in Janice's apartment and headed to the river with my fishing pole and some bits of the fish heads that I'd saved for the purpose of bait.

I didn't have quite as good luck at the river either that day. I caught only three blue gill and I would have to give one of those to Janice for keeping our stuff safe. That was okay, though; I still hoped I'd find a bird or two stuck in the pipe trap when I got back to the apartment building. When I got there, though, I found no birds, but all the grains of rice were gone. I was beginning to think that the trap didn't work or that someone else was stealing the birds that it had caught.

Sara wasn't home yet when I got back to the apartment after picking up our stuff and giving Janice her fish. To keep myself busy instead of worrying, I prepared the fish for cooking. Sara came in carrying a shopping bag, just as I was putting the fish in the oven to cook. I was so happy to see her, but that feeling faded as I noticed her appearance. She looked a little disheveled and her eyes seemed sadder and more haunted than ever. Her words of the night before, *I've gotta do whatever it takes to help us survive*, sprung to my mind and I was instantly alarmed at what she might have had to do today.

— *What happened?*

— *Nothing.*

Her voice sounded flat.

— *Come on. I know something's wrong. You can tell me, you know.*

— *Yeah, I know.*

Abruptly, she changed the subject and started pulling things out of the bag to show me. Her expression brightened somewhat, but I could tell something was still troubling her.

— *Look. I got seeds: lettuce, carrots, cucumbers, spinach, tomatoes. And look at this: I got a lockset so we can replace the lock on our door and keep our stuff here.*

— *Hmm, that's cool. Do you know how to do it?*

— *No, but it has instructions. We'll figure it out. I got a couple of screwdrivers.*

— *How'd you get all that? Was it in the food cache?*

— *No, Jason's parents own a hardware store. Well, I guess Jason owns it now. Anyway, the food cache is in the basement.*

Today he let me go upstairs and shop for some stuff we needed. The windows and doors of the store are all boarded up, so it hasn't been looted.

— He just let you have it?

— No...

When she saw the worried look on my face, she quickly added,

— I gave him one of my hundred dollar bills.

Something in her voice sounded a little off. Like maybe she was upset about having to give him so much money. Or maybe she was lying. That thought bothered me more than her paying him so much. Maybe she gave him something much more precious. I didn't want to think about it, so instead I took the lockset from her and started looking at it. As I concentrated on it, a thought came to my mind.

— Maybe we should look at the other apartments and see if we can find a better one.

— Why? I like this one.

— Well, maybe there's a two-bedroom, so I can have a bed to sleep in. And maybe we could find one with a microwave and more stuff.

— Okay. Maybe we should get one on

the top floor so we can keep an eye on the roof and our garden and traps and stuff.

— Good idea. Let's go check them out. We can go up and plant your seeds, too.

Sara smiled at that and for a few seconds the haunted look left her eyes. I was pleased that I was able to make her happy, if only for a moment.

Chapter 13

Surviving

The apartment building had six floors and the top floor was completely unoccupied. We found a two-bedroom apartment across the hall from the stairway that led to the roof. Luckily, this apartment had a microwave, quite a few pots and pans, a large bookcase full of books, and even closets and dressers full of clothes. Maybe its previous owners had died or hadn't wanted to come back to get their stuff after the fire. In either case, we felt lucky to have found it. Of course, we could have gone to each apartment and raided them to add to our stuff, but that seemed somehow wrong—like stealing or depriving someone else of the chance to survive.

We worked on changing the locks all the next morning. It was a bit of a struggle, trying to follow the instructions that came with the lockset, but we finally got it figured out. We felt such a sense of accomplishment that we celebrated that evening by eating two cans of vegetables and the last can of peaches for dinner. Afterwards, we went to the roof to plant Sara's seeds. She planted one row of carrots, one of spinach, one of lettuce, and the last one of cucumbers. She planted the tomato seeds in a large pot of soil she had found in the apartment with a dead houseplant in it and I had carried up to the roof for her. There were lots of seeds left over from each pack and these she carefully saved. After she was done planting, I helped her carry up pots of water to thoroughly wet the soil.

In the meantime, I worked on perfecting my bird trap. Instead of laying it on its side, I stood it up and wedged it between the parts of a huge air conditioning unit. I put several grains of rice in the bottom of it and hoped that birds would be lured down into it. I reasoned that the smooth sides wouldn't allow them to climb back out and it was too narrow to spread their wings to fly. I was happy that I could keep a watch over who went up to the roof through the peephole on our apartment door, so that I could be sure that no one was messing with our stuff on the roof. At least, when we were home.

Sara and I were proud and pleased with our accomplishments that day. It seemed that we were in control of our lives and I felt, for the first time in ages, that it was possible for me to gain an advantage over Time. School was supposed to start in two weeks and we would not be able to be out on the streets during the day, so having a way to survive without leaving the apartment was vital. We would have at least two months, though, before some of the vegetables Sara planted would be ready for harvest, according to the packages of seed, so a few trips to Jason's stash would be unavoidable.

The next morning, I woke early with the sun streaming through my east-facing bedroom windows. I hadn't had that problem with the other apartment, which was on the opposite side of the building. I tried to pull my pillow over my eyes and go back to sleep, but it was no use—I was too excited about life for the first time in a long time, so I jumped out of bed and pulled on my clothes. Sara was apparently still asleep so I decided to check on my bird trap, thinking that maybe the old saying, *the early bird gets the worm*, was true, although in this case, I was trying to get the bird.

As I neared the door, pulling on my shoes as I went, I heard footsteps in the hallway. Thinking it odd for someone to be clear up on the sixth floor this early in the morning, I peered through the peephole. It took a few seconds for the person to come into view and a few more for my eyes to adjust to the strange distortion of the viewer. I could tell the person was a man and that he looked vaguely familiar, but it wasn't until he paused at the door to the roof and looked around furtively, that I realized it was Gerald. By the time I had finished putting on my shoes, he had disappeared through the door to the roof. I slipped out of the apartment, checking to make sure I had the key and being careful to lock the door behind me so that Sara could sleep safely.

I followed Gerald, being as quiet as I could. I don't know why I felt the need to be secretive. Something about his manner made me suspicious, although I didn't know what I could possibly be distrustful of. Nevertheless, I hid behind the door at the top of the stairwell, cracking it open just a bit so I could see what Gerald was doing. At first he seemed confused, looking around for something that obviously wasn't where it should have been. It dawned on me that he was looking where I had originally placed my bird trap.

I watched Gerald scurry all over the roof

until he finally found the pipe stuck in the air conditioning unit. He had a silly grin on his face as he looked into the pipe, then reached in and pulled out a plump, blue-black Grackle, which began squawking loudly. Its panicked cries stopped abruptly, as Gerald wrung its neck with a quick flick of his hand.

I thought about leaving then and just letting him have the bird—after all, he was kind enough to let us remain, unharassed, in the building—but the thought of being able to provide meat for Sara, bringing forth that proud smile from her beautiful lips, was enough to change my mind, and I stepped out of the doorway. Gerald looked up, startled, then smiled as he stuffed the bird into a crumpled plastic grocery bag he had pulled out of his pocket.

— *Oh hi, Ben. You're up early.*

— *Yeah, I was just coming up to check on my bird trap. I guess you beat me to it.*

I tried to look perturbed, but either Gerald didn't notice or he chose to ignore it.

— *Oh? Where's that?*

— *That pipe over there where you found the bird.*

— *I'm not following you. How is a random pipe "your" bird trap?*

I pulled the pipe out of the crevice and showed Gerald the wire mesh. I also tipped it over and a few grains of rice dribbled out into my hand. I stared at him, challenging him to deny that I had made and baited it. He simply smiled again.

— *Ah, so it is. I didn't notice all that before. Well, here: I guess this is yours then.*

I hadn't expected him to give it up so easily and it caught me a little off guard. I didn't quite believe his claim that he hadn't noticed the construction, since it had been quite visible when it was laid flat on the roof, but I let it go.

— *That's okay. You can keep that one, but in the future…*

— *Of course. Now that I know it's yours, I'll leave the birds for you and Sara.*

He smiled again as he held up the bag.

— *Thanks for the bird.*

I nodded and smiled slightly back. He quickly changed the subject.

— *Speaking of Sara, how is she? I haven't seen her around much lately.*

— *We've been staying in our room mostly. Trying to avoid trouble. She got some seeds from Jason—I mean Sonny—and planted some vegetables in that pallet there.*

I wanted Gerald to know without a

doubt that the pallet garden belonged to us as well. Gerald looked at it, intrigued.

— *I wondered what that was. How ingenious.*

He peered at me intensely then and I felt like his eyes were piercing into my soul.

— *What'd she have to do to get seeds?*

His words seemed innocent enough, but the way he said them implied something dirty and I was struck by a sudden thrust of anger and jealousy. I spat out my next words from between my teeth.

— *What do you mean by that?*

— *Calm down, son. I didn't mean anything by it; just, well, you know—a girl that pretty...*

Gerald was doing some serious back-pedaling, trying to make amends, but I wasn't going to cut him any slack. I just kept staring at him, concentrating on shooting venom out of my eyes at him.

— *Look, son, sooner or later, her beauty's going to be a liability, you know, especially with all the gangs hanging around downtown. Sometime someone's gonna force her to do something she doesn't want to.*

I balled up my fists, thinking about punching Gerald, but something down inside me told me he was probably right, so I kept them by my side. While I stood rigid, trying to keep my anger in check, Gerald chose to leave. As he started toward the door, he turned back and offered me the bird with a look of sympathy.

— *Here, take this. Sara'll be real proud of you.*

When I refused to reach out and take it from his hand, he carefully laid it on the ground a few feet in front of me. Then he left without another word. I stood there for several minutes, fuming and thinking about what he'd said. It was undeniable that the thought had already entered my mind, but I had pushed it away every time. Now I was forced to face it with my heart pounding and my brain feeling like it was about to explode. After the rage started to subside, it was replaced by anguish and torment.

How was I going to keep her safe? I couldn't make her stay in the apartment all day, especially with the blistering summer heat coming soon. I couldn't even make her stay with me all the time—she would want to go to the food cache with Jason occasionally. I couldn't trust Jason to keep her safe; hell, I couldn't even be sure he wasn't already having his way with her. The memory of the sad, haunted look in her eyes the last time she returned from the cache seemed to give me the answer to the question that I hadn't even wanted to ask in the first place. I was ashamed of my cowardice.

Now that the question was forced upon me, I had to find the answer to it. I knew Sara would just deny everything, so I decided to confront Jason later that morning. Even though Sara kept saying he was a nice guy, I never completely trusted him. It would be a little difficult to get Jason alone to talk to him, as Sara was almost always with one or the other of us. I knew I should take advantage of the time alone right then to try to set things straight with him. At that moment, however, all I felt was a sudden and total exhaustion, like all the adrenalin that surged through my veins in anger a few moments before was immediately drained from my body, leaving me feeling weak and hopeless.

I dragged myself off the roof and went back to bed, leaving the bird where it lay and ignoring Time once again.

Chapter 14
Suspicion

Later that morning, Sara woke me up with a concerned look on her beautiful face. The sun was well up by then and it was getting hot in the apartment even though the windows were open. I hadn't realized that I had been asleep that long.

— *Are you okay, Ben?*

— *Yeah, just tired, I guess.*

— *I thought we might go down to the river today since it's so hot.*

I perked up immediately at the thought of spending the day at the river with her instead of alone. I felt much happier than just a few hours before. I smiled and jumped out of bed.

— *Yeah, that'd be nice.*

We took our fishing gear in a gym bag, happy that we could leave the rest of our stuff locked in our apartment and therefore would not have to share any of our catch with Janice. We walked hand in hand as we rounded the corner of the apartment building with big smiles on both our faces. We stopped short, however, at the sight of a police car driving slowly down the street toward us.

Our first instinct was to run, but I was sure that would just make the cops suspicious and cause them to chase us, so we decided to play it cool and just keep walking down the sidewalk toward the river. The cruiser slowed down and pulled over beside us. The officer in the passenger seat leaned out the window and called to me.

— *Hey, aren't you Ethan Michaels' son?*

I answered nervously.

— *Yeah.*

It was Officer Ortiz. I wasn't sure if that would help us or hurt us that he knew me and my background.

— *Did you ever find your dad after the fire?*

— *Yeah, he was okay.*

I decided to lie so Officer Ortiz wouldn't suspect that I was an orphan. Sara looked at me questioningly, but stayed silent.

— *Oh, good. I worried about you after that night. You looked pretty lost when I last saw you.*

I smiled to show my appreciation of his concern for me even though inside I still held it against him that he didn't try harder to save my dad.

— *What are you guys doing downtown? It isn't safe here, you know.*

— *My girlfriend wanted me to show her the destruction of the fire.*

— *Well, you should really be getting out of here now. There's been a lot of gang activity since the prisons were forced to release all the inmates after PF Day— looting, assaults, rapes, even murders. In fact, a girl was murdered day before yesterday just a few blocks from here. I'm telling you, it ain't safe out here. You better be getting home.*

Sara glanced at me with a startled look in her eyes, but looked away quickly. Was that fear I saw in her eyes or some sort of guilt? I couldn't help thinking it was the latter. I stared at her for a few moments before I realized that Officer Ortiz was waiting for me to respond.

— *We were heading home just now.*

— *Where do you live?*

— *Up north, across the river.*

Officer Ortiz leaned back in and consulted with his partner about something.

After a few seconds, he leaned back out the window to talk to us again.

— *I was going to offer you guys a ride, but Henry says we got orders to continue south.*

— *That's okay. It's not too far.*

— *Well you two be careful. Stay on the main roads and don't stop until you get home, okay?*

— *Yes sir.*

The officers drove off, leaving me to wonder about Sara's strange reaction to the grim news we had just been given. I took her hand and pulled her around to face me.

— *What was that all about?*

— *What do you mean?*

— *That look you gave me after he told us about the murder.*

— *I don't know. It just freaked me out, I guess.*

Sara seemed prickly and defensive. It just didn't add up in my mind. What did she have to feel guilty and defensive about? Unless she had something to do with it. A sick feeling started in the pit of my stomach, and then got worse after I realized what I was suspecting her of. I had to find out.

— *You're acting weird, like you're guilty or something.*

— Guilty?

Sara's voice got angry and loud as she continued,

— What do you think I am? Some kind of murderer or something? How could you think that?

She yanked her hand out of mine and started walking fast. I jogged to catch up to her and when I did, I could see her wiping tears off her cheeks.

— Hey, I'm sorry. I didn't mean it the way it sounded. Of course I don't think you're a murderer.

— Just leave me alone!

Her voice was thin and shrill. She broke into a run to try to distance herself from me. I could tell that I had hurt her feelings. I cursed myself under my breath as I ran to catch up with her again.

— Sara, please slow down. I didn't mean it, really. Please believe me. I'm an idiot. Please, Sara.

I was pleading with her by then. I reached out and grabbed her hand and she let me use it to stop her and draw her to me. She buried her face in my shoulder and started sobbing, her entire body shaking in my arms. We stood there like that for several minutes and it occurred to me that this seemed an extreme reaction for the situation. Things still didn't add up, but I'd learned my lesson about sticking my foot in my mouth, so I said nothing more about it.

We walked on to the river in silence. I was now worried about these murderous gangs that Officer Ortiz had told us about and I was constantly looking around us as we walked. For the second time that day, my adrenalin level was elevated and I felt as jumpy as one of the stray cats or dogs that had become fair game for starving people in the past few months. We made it to the river without incident but were too bummed out to fish or enjoy the day, so we headed home after a half hour or so.

The rest of the afternoon Sara had that haunted look in her eyes but this time, something else was lurking there. Fear, anguish, guilt? It was killing me to find out what was bothering her, but I didn't dare ask. I couldn't risk making her feel bad again and pushing her away like I had my mother. Neither one of us felt like talking so we each picked out a book off the bookshelf and sat in the living room reading and trying to keep our minds off what had happened.

That night, as she headed toward her room to go to bed, Sara suddenly turned to me and started talking, like she had a secret that she just couldn't keep in any longer.

— *I didn't kill that girl, Ben.*

— *I know you didn't.*

— *But I know who did.*

She shook her head sadly as my eyes nearly popped out of my head in alarm and the question *Who?* formed on my lips. Without answering, she went into her bedroom and shut the door.

Chapter 15
Revelation

Sara and I stayed in the apartment building for the next couple of weeks, spending most of our time on the roof in the shade of the dormant air conditioning unit. We were afraid to leave the building both because of the threat of gang activity and the possibility of being picked up by police and sent to foster homes. School had started a few days before and we wanted no part of that scene.

We took a couple of chairs up to sit on and even dragged the mattress from my bed up there to sleep on at night. We had most of our meager meals up there as well, mostly birds and an occasional rat or mouse we were able to trap. We were hungry most of the time, but at least we had water, a toilet, and most important of all, freedom.

Most of the time, the other residents of the apartment building left us alone. There were always new people coming to the building and then moving out after a day or two, never wanting to stay in one place very long. Gerald stayed off the roof, probably because he didn't want to confront me again. Occasionally, Jason would come to the roof to visit, but never stayed long since I was still quite cool toward him.

The first night we slept on the roof I tried to get romantic with Sara, since we were now sleeping together, but she pushed me away and rolled over to face away from me.

— *Please don't, Ben. Everyone always wants a piece of me. That's why I stay with you; you never try to force me into doing anything I don't want to do. I feel safe with you. Please don't ruin it now.*

As much as I wanted Sara right then, having her stay with me was much more important, so I kept my hands to myself from then on. I kept hoping she'd change her mind and initiate some contact, but it never happened. I buried the disappointment of my desire deep down inside me with all the other pain I was hiding. It wasn't that hard to ignore my physical desires; I felt like I was emotionally dead anyway and the strain of trying to keep all that buried exhausted me physically as well.

One night just after dark, Jason came

staggering up the stairs to the roof. He was a mess, his nose bloody and a black eye already forming. He was dragging his left leg and hugging his chest. His wheezing reminded me of my dad after he had been beaten in the riot for water months before. Despite my dislike and distrust of him, I couldn't help feeling a surge of concern and pity for the poor guy. Sara was stricken with concern, almost making me jealous. She ran to his side.

— *Jason! What happened?*

Jason was unable to speak right away. It was several minutes after Sara had helped him to a chair before he could tell us what happened. What he said chilled me to the bone.

—*They're looking for you, Sara. Your brother and your ex and their gang. You have to leave.*

I'll never forget the look on Sara's face—a mix of terror, concern, and panic. I felt the adrenalin surge through my veins and I was stricken with the same feelings I saw in Sara's face. I also felt intense anger toward Jason, which I unleashed with a verbal assault.

— *You dumb ass! You probably led them here to her! How could you put her in danger like that? I ought to beat the crap out of you right now!*

I didn't expect to see the intense dejection and self-loathing in Jason's face and it cooled my anger immediately. Sara shot me an angry look of warning, which cooled it even more. What Jason said next almost made me feel sorry for him.

— *I know. I couldn't think straight. I don't think they were following me, though. I've been out cold in the alley behind the hardware store since this morning.*

Sara told me to go down to the apartment and bring up wet rags and any kind of medicine and bandages I could find. It took me a few minutes to collect the items, during which time my mind was spinning with panic, trying to settle on a plan to keep Sara safe. By the time I returned to the roof, I had decided that it would probably be safest to stay where we were instead of trying to run through streets that were controlled by rogue gangs, one of them being the ones looking for her. As Sara cleaned up Jason as best she could and bandaged his bruised and possibly broken ribs and foot, I explained what I had decided. Jason argued a little, but Sara was silent. She didn't speak much until after we had helped Jason down to his apartment, making him as comfortable as we could, and returned to the roof with several cans of food that Jason gave us for helping him. As we shut the door on his apartment, I made sure to turn the lock so he would be safe. Sara smiled at me for that and I felt selfless and good about myself for once.

When we got to the roof, I blocked the door by forcing two metal bars through the handrails on each side of the door. For extra measure, Sara helped me push a heavy drum of some unknown substance in front of the door. We lay down on the mattress and pulled our blanket over us, but neither of us could sleep. We didn't talk for a long time, but finally I couldn't hold it in any longer.

— *So are you going to tell me about your brother?*

I wanted to ask about her ex as well, but decided not to push it. It was a minute or so before Sara answered.

— *Matthew is four years older than me. Last year, or maybe it was the year before— I've lost track of the time—he started hanging out with a bad bunch of guys. Drinking, drugs, and such. He was always getting into trouble and getting suspended from school. Of course, that's exactly what he wanted so he could go hang out with the other druggies. My parents tried and tried to straighten him out. I felt so bad for them. I hated my brother for putting them through all that. At the same time, though, I still loved him. You know what I mean?*

I nodded but said nothing, afraid that she would quit talking if I said anything. She sighed then, a deep, sad sigh.

— *I had this boyfriend, Zack. We weren't serious or anything, but I liked him. Matthew started luring him to hang out with his gang. Zack was only 15, but he got into the drugs just like my brother. One night they were arrested for being in a big fight with some other guys. They all had drugs on them and they all ended up going to jail, Zack to juvie, but Matthew was charged as an adult since he was 18 and got three to five years. I guess they had to let them out when the power was off.*

I was silent for a couple of minutes more, then I asked what I'd been dying to know for days.

— *So, how do you know who killed that girl? Was it your brother or one of his gang?*

She took so long to answer I thought she'd gone to sleep, but she finally spoke.

This time her voice was thin and wavering like she was trembling or trying not to cry.

— I saw Matthew and Zack the first time I went with Jason, when we were coming back home. Zack was trying to get me to go with him, to be his "ho." He got mad when I said no. Jason told them I was his girlfriend and that he would give them food if they left us alone. He gave them all the food he had in his backpack. It worked; they let us go. The next time I saw them was when I got the seeds. It was late and Jason still had to board the store back up behind us. I came back alone because I was worried about you worrying about me. Zack had this sick-looking girl hanging on him. She looked like she'd been beat up pretty bad. Like she was almost dead already. He still tried to get me to go with him and when I refused again, he got real mad. The girl tried to say that he only needed her and that made him even madder. He punched her in the stomach real hard and she started throwing up blood. I tried to run away, but Matthew caught me and threatened to kill me if I ever told anyone what I saw. I gave him a hundred dollars and he let me go. Jason never asked for anything from me; it was Matthew I paid. When I looked back, the girl was lying

on the ground in a pool of blood, already dead, I suppose.

At that, Sara's voice cracked and she started crying. I pulled her close and let her cry into my shoulder. She kept murmuring over and over, *that poor girl* until she fell asleep in my arms. I stayed awake, worrying about the gang, the threat to Sara, and thinking about how wrong I'd been to judge Jason without knowing the facts. It made me wonder how many other times I had jumped to conclusions about someone before knowing the whole story. I put the headphones of Sara's iPod in my ears and finally drifted off to sleep with the soft sounds of *Mad World* and visions of my mother's sad and disappointed face haunting my dreams.

Chapter 16
Escape

Muffled pounding and shouting downstairs awakened us during the night. At first I thought it was part of the music still playing in my ear, but when I heard a woman scream, I sat bolt upright, accidentally pulling the headphones out of my ears. In the dim light of a sliver of the moon, Sara's eyes were huge pools of fear. She clutched at me and whispered, panic making her voice tremble,

— *It's them!*

For a moment, we just sat there blinking, but when a second scream, this time a male voice, wailed on long and anguished, finally weakening to a strangled moan, I jumped into action. I started stuffing all our things into our two gym bags, which we kept on the roof with us. Sara stood and quietly helped. Her movements seemed stiff and slow and made me think of the phrase "scared stiff." I stopped for a moment and held her close until she calmed down a little.

The voices were sounding louder, like they were working their way up the floors. We were startled by a sound like a gunshot, but we couldn't believe anyone would still have ammunition left after all this time. We weren't taking any chances, though, and went back to packing with additional urgency. When we were done, we slung the bags on our backs and carefully made our way to the burned out section of the building where we knew there was, ironically, a fire escape.

Hoping the fire hadn't weakened the metal too much, we started down the stairs, testing each step while still trying to hurry. About halfway down, we heard pounding on the door to the roof. We paused only a moment, and then continued. We were on the last landing before the final flight, which ended about eight feet off the ground, when the shadow of a man rounded the corner on our side of the building. We froze and prayed that he would not think to look up. We could barely see him, the dim moonlight reflecting off his bald head, as he stopped under the fire escape and turned his face up toward us. I could feel Sara's muscles tighten and I feared that the man would hear the sound of my heart beating wildly in my chest.

Apparently, his eyes hadn't adjusted to the darkness yet, having just came out of the now brightly-lit building, because he just squinted for several seconds, then turned and yelled at his gang that nobody was on this side of the building. We didn't move until we heard the door to the back of the building open and close again. Then we quickly dropped to the ground from the bottom rung, grabbed hands and started running as quietly as we could across the street to the alley between the buildings to the east. We could hear more shouting as the gang exited the back of our building and I swear I heard them calling for Sara.

We rushed eastward as fast as we dared, pausing at the corners before darting across the open territory of the streets. We ran for at least ten blocks before we were so out of breath we had to hide in a recessed doorway to rest for a minute. As we caught our breath, Sara looked at me with her huge, haunted eyes, which were clouded by fear as well. I tried to look reassuringly back at her, but I'm not sure I was able to pull it off convincingly. Wordlessly, we continued east until we hit a major boulevard running north and south. I stopped Sara in the middle of a clump of trees and we silently listened for the sound of someone following us. After several long seconds, I whispered,

— *Which way should we go?*

— *South.*

She said it with such conviction that I didn't think to argue with her. I was curious what she had in mind, though. She started walking briskly south. I had to hurry a little to catch up to her. We stayed at the edge of the trees that lined the side of the boulevard.

— *Why south?*

— *Swope Park.*

— *Swope Park?*

I'd never been to Swope Park before, except to visit the zoo.

— *Yeah, it has a big woods and a river that runs through it. And the zoo's there.*

— *Why would we want to go to the zoo at a time like this?*

She looked at me like I was a bit slow.

— *Animals... hunting...?*

She smiled slightly when it dawned on me that she was far ahead of me in thinking about survival. If there were any animals left in the zoo by now, that is. At any rate, the idea of hiding in the woods by a river was very appealing to me after being cooped up in the apartment building so much, especially since summer was coming on and we wouldn't have been able to run the air conditioners in the building.

We walked for the rest of the night until dawn, probably three hours or so. By the time we made it to Swope Park, we were exhausted. At the first bridge crossing the Blue River, we left the road and scrambled down the steep hill to the riverbanks below. The river was really just a stream, only about ten or twelve feet across. We settled under the bridge, using our gym bags as pillows and fell asleep.

While I slept, I dreamed that a huge beast was after us. In the darkness of my mind, we ran through the streets of downtown with the monster on our heels. We couldn't see what it was; we could only see its glowing yellow eyes and hear its roar. Right before I woke up, I dreamed we rounded the corner of a building and there in front of us, strewn on the street under a streetlight were the bodies of Gerald, Janice, and Skinner. The beast was hunched over another body with its back to us. As we stood and stared, horrified, the body under the beast raised its head and looked at us with wounded, accusing eyes. It was Jason.

I woke with a start, overwhelmed by

feelings of guilt and remorse—remorse for treating Jason badly, guilt for leaving him behind to face the gang alone. And what about Janice and Gerald? They'd been kind to us when we needed them. Shouldn't I have stayed to help them in their time of need? I shook my head and decided that there was nothing I could have done. My first duty was to Sara and I couldn't have protected her if I'd gone downstairs to help the others. Nonetheless, the bad feelings stayed with me all day.

Another thing that stayed with me during the day was the sound of the beast roaring; only now I realized that it was a real beast roaring from the nearby zoo. Sara said it was a lion and he sounded forlorn and hungry. It scared me, but Sara was excited by the sound. She wanted to sneak into the zoo after we had found something to eat and see if there were any other animals left. I wasn't too sure about that.

— *What if they eat us?*

— *They can't get out of their pens, silly. Most of them are probably dead anyway. No way to get food for them when so many people are starving and probably no one to take care of them either.*

Sara seemed quite saddened by that

thought, but I was glad there wouldn't be many animals around to try to eat us. I hadn't been to the zoo since my kindergarten field trip years before, but I remembered big scary beasts like lions, tigers, and polar bears. I wasn't too keen on meeting up with one of them, particularly since they were undoubtedly hungry.

Chapter 17
Swope Park

Fishing under the bridge was good, so we quickly caught two large catfish. We decided we needed to move upriver, away from the sight of the road, before we made a fire and cooked them. We walked along the railroad tracks that roughly followed the flow of the river. About a half a mile up and around a bend in the river, we came upon an abandoned train on the tracks. We could see and smell wisps of smoke rising above a clump of trees ahead of us. We hesitated, not sure whether the fire-builder would be friendly or not.

Cautiously, we peeked around a large tree and watched while a dark and wrinkled old man tended to a spit holding some kind of meat suspended over the fire. The body of the animal was freshly skinned and apparently hadn't been cooking long enough to brown the meat or give off an aroma. Sara and I glanced at each other and somehow agreed to reveal ourselves without uttering a word. As usual, Sara was the first to speak to the man, sounding very courteous and respectful.

— *Good morning, sir. We were wondering if we could share your fire for a bit.*

He eyed us suspiciously and cocked his head to the side.

— *There ain't enough for more than me. Best you leave me be an' find your own food.*

— *We don't want to take your food, sir. We have our own. See?*

Sara grabbed my hand and held it and the fish aloft.

— *Well, in that case, sure, you can share my fire.*

The man relaxed and nodded toward the fire.

— *Thank you, sir.*

— *What be your names?*

— *I'm Sara and this is Ben.*

— *Nice to meet you Sara an' Ben. You can call me Aaron. Why don't you pull up a rock there an' dress your fish. Might be good to find a long green stick to roast 'em on too.*

Aaron's voice was deep and musical. In my scarred heart, I felt I could trust this man, even though my brain told me to trust nobody but Sara. Apparently, Sara felt comfortable around him as well, because she smiled and relaxed for the first time in days. She seemed to enjoy the conversation she was having with Aaron.

— *Thanks, Aaron. It's been awhile since I roasted something over a campfire.*

— *Your boy there don't talk much. Is he mute or just shy?*

I felt the heat of embarrassment warm my cheeks as I realized how rude I'd been. I smiled sheepishly.

— *I can talk. I'm just quiet, I guess.*

— *Well, that's awright, Ben. I can talk enough for the both of us. I'm named after Aaron, Moses' brother, in the Bible. Ever hear of him? Well, ol' Moses, he weren't a very good speaker, so God told him to speak through his brother Aaron when he needed to tell that ol' pharaoh in Egypt off. God told Moses what to say an' Moses told Aaron what God said to say. Kinda like Sara here doin' the talking for both of you.*

Aaron chuckled at his little joke and turned the spit a quarter turn. While Sara carried on the conversation with Aaron, I set to work dressing the fish and finding long sticks to roast them on. I listened carefully to what they were saying, however.

— So what are you two doin' down here on the Little Blue? Don't you have a home?

— We did, but we got burned out of them. Both Ben's and my parents died and we didn't want to end up in foster homes. We're almost seventeen anyway, so we can be emancipated soon.

— Well now. Emancipation is something I know a little bit about.

He smiled mysteriously and turned the spit again.

Just then, the lion roared again, this time long and mournful. It sounded so much closer, even though we had only walked a half a mile or so upriver. I started at the sound, visions of the beast attacking us from the woods next to us in my head, as I commented,

— Damn, that sounds close.

Aaron nodded his head sympathetically.

— His pen is right across the river an' up that hill. His voice can carry for miles, but we're less than half a mile away here. He sounds real lonesome, doesn't he?

Sara said sadly,

— I feel sorry for him. Is he all alone now? Didn't they have, like, five or six lions before?

— Yep. They've all died but the one.

Died of exposure or sickness. The last one ate his brothers to survive.

We all shuddered in horror at the thought of the dire hunger that led him to devour his pride.

— *The keepers tried to keep all the animals alive, but it was a losing battle.*

— *The keepers? They stayed while the power was out? Was the zoo even open?*

— *No, no, the zoo closed the day of the power failure an' probly ain't never gonna open up again. Most of the staff decided they needed to be home with their families, of course, helping them survive. But there are five dedicated keepers, who have no families of their own. These five have stayed all through the crisis. See that building up yonder?*

Aaron pointed a ways up the tracks to a building.

— *That's where they live now. They tried living in the buildings at the zoo at first, but the stench drove them away.*

— *Stench?*

Aaron shook his head and turned away, like he didn't really want to think about it. It took him a few seconds, but when he answered, his voice was husky and sad.

— *The dead animals.*

We were all silent for a few minutes, during which time, Sara and I began roasting our fish. It didn't take them long to cook and we immediately devoured them while Aaron ate his own lunch. Afterwards, we cleaned up the campsite a little. Aaron snapped a green branch covered with leaves off a nearby tree and used it to tamp out the flames of the fire. After it was out, he opened one of the train cars' sliding doors, grabbed a huge shovel from inside, and carefully scooped up the hot coals from the fire. He laid the coals, still on the shovel, inside the train car. Then he pulled out four large plastic buckets and climbed the ladder attached to the outside of the train car to the roof, setting the buckets on the rooftop. When he saw me looking at him quizzically, he explained his actions.

— *It looks a little dark to the west. It might rain later. Gotta make sure we have the makin's for a fire later an' rainwater is always better for drinkin' than river water.*

I was amazed at his foresight and efficiency. I realized that Aaron would probably be a great source of information if Sara and I were going to survive in the woods for the winter. If he would let us stay with him, that is. Aaron got out some fishing line, a bucket,

143

and a knife. He surprised me with a great display of enthusiasm.

— *Time for fishin'!*

— *Why? We just ate.*

— *You don't wait 'til you're hungry to find your next meal, son. Besides, if rain's a-comin', the fish'll be a-bitin'.*

— *How do you know?*

I didn't say it like a smart-ass; I was genuinely interested.

— *I been livin' in the wild for a long time, Ben. Every time before it rains, the fish want to eat as much as they can because the rain muddies up the water so they can't see the food. After it rains, you may as well not even try to fish.*

— *You don't have a fishing pole?*

— *No, I just have this string with my home-made hook. See? You can make a hook out of lots of things.*

Aaron showed me the hook he had made out of a pop can tab. He had cut part of one of the rings off to form the barb. A string was tried to the other ring. When we got down to the river, he pulled what looked like animal guts out of the pail and impaled a small piece on his homemade hook. He offered some to me for my hook.

— *Nothin' better than entrails for*

baitin' catfish!

We fished for about an hour and caught over a dozen fish, mostly catfish from Aaron's hook and specialized technique. I didn't know what in the world we would do with all those fish. Sara and I always ate what we caught almost immediately, but we were still full from our meal an hour before and I knew the fish wouldn't stay fresh too long. Aaron knew exactly what to do with them, however.

After we cleaned and gutted a little over half the fish, Aaron filleted them and cut the meat into long, thin strips; he left the other fish alive on a stringer in the river. After he had prepared the fish strips, he opened the sliding door of another freight car, which had open vents all over the sides of it. In this car was a rack made of tree limbs. Aaron had me gather green sticks for firewood while he and Sara hung the fish on the rack. He made a fire under the rack using the wood I had found and a live coal he had saved from earlier. Then he placed a big tripod, also made of tree limbs, over the rack and covered it with a blanket, like a teepee with an opening at the top for the smoke to escape and room at the bottom to draw in air. It took a while for the fire to catch on since the wood was green and after it did, it smoked a lot, which was exactly what Aaron wanted. He said it would take a couple of days to dry it out enough to be safe to eat without refrigeration.

Aaron closed the door to the "smoke-house" and went back to the river to retrieve the rest of the fish. The lion roared as if he knew that Aaron had fresh food.

— *Let's go see what's happenin' at the zoo.*

Chapter 18

City Zoo

We followed the river another half-mile until we came to a swinging bridge. Sara was excited when she saw it, remembering all the times she and her parents stood on the bridge making it sway back and forth. We scrambled up the steep bank to an opening in the chain link fence at the top. Sara delightedly demonstrated the effect of the bridge while I nervously looked around for possible loose animals. There was a foul stench in the air. I had smelled it a little down below in the river valley, but up here it was much stronger. Aaron saw me wrinkle my nose and shook his head sadly, saying only,

— *The stench of death.*

On our way to the lion's pen, we passed many empty enclosures. It was sad to think that so many animals had lost their lives because of PF Day. No more depressing, of course, than the loss of human lives, but sad, nonetheless. I hadn't even thought about the hardships faced by the animals in the zoo. After all, animals don't need electricity, right? But in captivity, totally dependent on humans to feed them, and dependent on food sources that are shipped in from other places, the loss of power had a devastating effect on them.

The few animals that were still alive were thin, mirroring the human population. The huge silverback gorilla and one of his mates had made it, but the other five gorillas had not. More than half of the African plains animals, like the zebras, giraffes, rhinoceros, and antelopes were still alive; none of the hippos made it, though. Two cheetahs were still alive, although very skinny, and all the tough little warthogs survived. Sara was afraid to continue to the chimpanzee enclosure—afraid that the baby chimp that she had loved to watch frolicking with his mother and siblings had died, but Aaron assured her that although some of the others had not made it, the baby was still among the living.

When we arrived at the lion's enclosure, he let out a low mournful roar, like he knew we were there to see him. First we entered the viewing room to see him, but it was so hot in there, we came back out to the side of it. Aaron told me to climb up on the top of the small building and after I did, he handed the fish up to me and told me to toss them to the lion.

Just before I threw them in, the lion's eyes locked on mine. His intense stare spooked me because it seemed like he was thinking that I was the food being offered to him that day. He crouched like he was ready to leap to the top of the building and make a meal out of me. His eyes had an eager gleam and his tongue licked his upper lip slowly in anticipation. I hurriedly tossed the fish to him, one by one, but his gaze didn't leave me until I hastily climbed back down off the roof. By the time I joined Sara and Aaron at the fence overlooking the enclosure, the lion was ripping into the fish like I had never been the object of his desire. However, I couldn't shake the eerie feeling of being pegged as prey.

We left the zoo after feeding the lion because the smell of rotting flesh and the sadness of the situation began to overwhelm Sara and me. After returning to the train, Aaron suggested we choose a car to sleep in. He said that there were several other homeless people who came back here at night after foraging for food in the city all day. They chose to sleep in the woods, though. We chose a freight car about halfway down the train that was half-filled with boxes of hardware items—big spools of wire, tools, paint, etc. We decided that it would be advantageous, from a survival standpoint, to search through the boxes to find items that would help us. The car next to that one was filled with boxes that appeared to be from some kind of veterinary supply company because there were boxes of vaccines, antibiotics, medicines, and such. There were even pet supplies in there and we spent the rest of the afternoon searching through boxes in both cars. We were happy to uncover a box of large flat pet beds in the pet car. We took several out and used them for our beds in the hardware car.

That night Aaron lit a big fire beside the train. Out of the darkness, people started sifting in from all sides. It reminded me of a zombie invasion the way they silently appeared from the woods or from behind the train, and it kind of creeped me out. I could tell Sara felt a little anxious too, because she dragged me down to the river to get away from them. I think she was still freaked out that her brother's gang might appear. I didn't blame her.

After a while, Aaron came down to the river to find us. He was carrying a bucket, a big branch lit on fire like a torch, and three long barbecue spits, the ones you roast hot dogs over a fire with. He handed one to each of us and told us that he was going to teach how to gig frogs. He showed us how to creep along the banks of the river, shining the torch in front of us. When we could see the light reflected off the eyeballs of a big bullfrog, he thrust the barbeque spit at it, impaling it. It took us a while to get the hang of it, but once we did we caught several. While we gigged, we talked softly. I had to ask Aaron the question that had been bothering Sara and me since nightfall.

— *Who are all those people at the campfire?*

— *Just folks. Folks that ain't got a home. Don't want one neither.*

— *What do you mean?*

— *They're just ... well, lost souls. Most of 'em were let out of the mental institutions after PF Day.*

— *Why would they just let them out? I mean, they're crazy, right?*

— *Well now, we're all just a little crazy, ain't we? Take you two. You could be at some nice person's home with electricity, hangin' out with your friends an' all but instead, you decide to hang out here with the crazies.*

Aaron started laughing loudly and laughed until he started coughing. When he caught his breath, he continued more seriously.

— Really, though, think about it. What were the authorities supposed to do? They couldn't leave 'em all in there to starve to death, to die of thirst or disease. Who was going to be there to take care of 'em? No, they had no choice but to let 'em all out. Prisoners too. That's why the city's a lot more dangerous now than before.

Sara and I glanced at each other. We knew firsthand how true that last statement was.

After we had caught a couple dozen frogs, we headed back to the fire. Aaron assured us that there were no gangs among the group. We were still apprehensive and stayed back by the trees until we looked everyone over. There were eight men and three women in the group, as far as we could tell. A few of them could have been either gender. They were all dressed pretty raggedy and obviously didn't fit the gang type, so we cautiously joined them around the fire. Aaron introduced us and the others told us their names.

We cut the fat legs off the frogs, skinned them, and roasted them over the fire. There were enough to share with everyone and the others gratefully devoured their share.

After a while, three men and two women joined the group. These five were obviously not homeless or mentally ill. You could just tell by the way they walked and talked. They were educated; they had a purpose. Aaron introduced them to us as the keepers of the zoo, who lived in the building down the tracks. They looked exhausted and grim, but their eyes lit up a bit when Aaron told them we were interested in the welfare of the zoo and the animals in it. One of the men, Jim, started to explain to us what they've been doing to help the animals since PF Day and how they had made the excruciating decisions they had to.

— *After PF Day, most of the zoo personnel came to work every day until the gas ran out. Those who had families naturally had to stay home to take care of them. There were eight of us, originally, who were able to stay to take care of the animals. Of course, at first we had no idea how long the power would be out, so we went about as usual, feeding the animals as we had always done. In some ways that was bad, but in other ways good. They were well fed and healthy as we headed into the winter. But we ran out of food to feed many of them halfway through the winter. We knew at that point the power was going to be off a long time.*

Jim paused and stared into the fire sadly. A middle-aged woman named Susan took up the account.

— *That's when we had to make some hard decisions. The zoo director and some of the board members were walking to the zoo from their homes about once a week at that time to check up on things. At one point we all decided that we would have to make a plan to keep as many animals alive as possible. First of all, we had to make a priority list of the animals that were most important to be kept alive and the ones most likely to survive.*

Another young keeper, Kyle, interrupted softly.

— *That was a difficult task.*

— *Yes, excruciating. But it had to be done. Obviously, the most endangered species had to have a high priority. We unanimously decided that the primates were a top priority because of their intelligence and most are endangered as well. The large carnivores like the polar bears, the big cats, and the wild dogs needed meat and the only way to provide that was for something else to die. I mean, another zoo animal. We couldn't very well be feeding them beef and pork when people were starving, you know. So the question was, should we kill lesser priority animals to feed higher priority carnivores? It turned out that we didn't have to because so many animals started dying quickly; so many we had too much meat to feed the carnivores at first. Luckily, the meat kept in the winter. By spring, though, we were running low on usable meat. Especially when the weather warmed up and the dead animals started rotting.*

Some of the mentally ill people around the fire began to look uneasy. A few of them got up and retreated into the woods, shaking their heads and muttering softly to themselves. They vanished as quickly as they had appeared earlier, reinforcing my impression of zombies.

Jim spoke again.

— *The penguins posed a particularly difficult problem. Many of them were endangered and a high priority for us to try to save, but feeding them and controlling the water temperature was impossible. You see, before PF Day the zoo brought in a truckload of fresh fish and seafood from the coasts every month to feed them. They don't eat anything else. The warm-water penguins couldn't recover from the cold temperatures either. Despite our best efforts, we lost all but two penguins last winter.*

Now Kyle entered the conversation.

— *We had already stored enough hay for the winter to keep most of the herbivores alive. We only lost one of the elephants and a few of the African plains herbivores. We suspect that a few of them were poached, but not as many as we thought would be.*

Sara and I glanced guiltily at each other. Even though we hadn't poached any of the animals, we had thought about it and now, after witnessing their terrible plight, we couldn't even imagine killing the ones who had managed to survive thus far.

— *We lost quite a few of the kangaroos, though. We're hoping that things will begin to get better soon, now that the electricity is back on. We won't give up on them, no matter what happens.*

Later that night, while Sara and I laid on our beds in the freight car, we talked about how terrible it must have been to make the decisions of which animals to save. Sara looked intensely at me and said,

— *You see, Ben; sometimes people have to make decisions they don't want to. What you think is a choice that somebody made willingly may have been just the best one of a bunch of terrible choices.*

Something about the way she said it made me think she had suddenly changed the subject.

— *Are you talking about the zookeepers?*

— *Yes... and others...*

She paused then. It seemed that she wanted to say something else, but I didn't want to hear it so I turned away and told her I was tired.

Chapter 19
Wilderness Survival

The summer and fall were filled with learning valuable survival techniques from Aaron, the keepers, and even a few of the mentally ill people who frequented our campsite. As it had for the past several months, Time seemed to stand still for us, even though it had been restored to the rest of the world through the repair of the power grid. We, however, lived as though the power was still off; electricity held no interest for us, except to recharge Sara's iPod at one of the picnic grounds' outlets from time to time.

We were able to find many items from the freight cars to help with our survival and make our lives easier. We tried to help the homeless people who, even though they had lived around the train for several months, had not felt comfortable entering the cars to scavenge. Aaron said that most of them were too paranoid to sleep within any kind of enclosure and that quite a bit of their mental problems were actually caused, or at least made worse, by confining them in mental institutions. He worried that it was only a matter of time before the authorities started rounding them up again to institutionalize them for "their own good." Aaron almost spat out those last three words; there was no question what he thought about the prospect.

We made the train our home base for the next few months. We slept inside the car when it was cool or raining and on top of it when the temperatures soared. The trees shaded our car and a few others around it during the day so the metal never got too hot. On especially hot nights, we brought buckets of water from the river to cool down the roof and ourselves.

We had some intestinal problems due to bacteria and parasites in the water before Aaron told us to boil buckets of river water for drinking. He made us a tonic from the stinging nettle plant to help detox our system.

During the days, Aaron showed us various techniques for trapping animals. He taught us how to make snares from a piece of wire and where to place them on animal trails for catching small game. He showed us how to set up pitfall traps and bucket traps.

He even showed us how to dam up a small section of the river or a creek to catch fish. Then he demonstrated how to correctly skin and gut the animals we caught and how to preserve some for eating later. For every two animals we ate, we tried to preserve at least one by smoking and drying it out like jerky.

Aaron also knew all about edible plants. He showed us how to find and use cattails, which he called the grocery store of the wild. Most of its parts are edible: the young shoots and stems taste like cucumber, the flower spikes like corn on the cob, and the rhizomes can be made into flour. Aaron was careful to show us the difference between cattails and its poisonous look-alike, the blue flag iris, which has leaves separate from the stalk, unlike cattail whose leaves sheathe the stalk.

We also learned how to identify and collect lamb's quarters, dandelion leaves, and nettles for a wild salad and many wild berries and fruits. We collected pine needles to make pine needle tea, which Aaron told us contains four times the vitamin C of orange juice. By the end of summer, we were feeling quite confident in our ability to survive in the wild. Aaron taught us that survival is about finding solutions to your problems. He would always say that people who sit around and cry over their problems usually don't survive.

Two or three days a week, we went to the zoo and helped the keepers care for the animals that were still holding on to life. Some of the pens and enclosures had bodies of fresh water available to the animals, but others had to be supplied by carrying buckets of water. It seemed a never-ending task and it sounds heartless, but I was glad that there were fewer animals to be taken care of. It was quite a bit easier after the keepers were able to get some gas to run their tractors and ATVs, although there were always dead animals that needed to be butchered to feed the carnivores and plants to be gathered for the herbivores. In return for our help, the keepers taught us veterinary care which, they reminded us, could be used on humans as well, and shared some of the butchered meat with us. It seemed odd eating exotic animals, like kudu and wild boar, but after cooking them over a fire, they all tasted pretty similar in the end.

Sometime in late summer—we had no idea what day, as there was no reason for us to keep track of time—two men from the railroad came walking up the tracks from where they had parked their company truck on the side of the nearest road. Sara and I hid in the woods while Aaron talked to them. One of them questioned him, while the other checked the engine over.

— *Anybody living in this train?*

— *A few lost souls is all.*

— *Well, the railroad sent us to check out the condition of this train. I'm afraid we'll be getting it ready to move soon. Tell all your people to get their belongings and whatever they need out of here in the next few days. We'll be back here with the engineers on Friday to start it up and drive it out of here.*

We could tell that the men were kind and concerned about the future living conditions of the "lost souls." We were worried that they would report us to authorities who would no doubt determine that the best thing for us would be to gather us up and send us to various "appropriate" institutions, like psych wards, prisons, orphanages, and schools. There was no way any of us wanted that and now that we had freedom, we were determined to do anything it took to keep it.

For the next three days, we unloaded anything we thought might help us survive out of the freight cars and carried it to secret caches deep in the woods. We made the caches by burying several large plastic trashcans from the hardware car of the train in various places throughout the heavily wooded areas of the park. The lids were level with the ground and we camouflaged them with leaves, sticks, rocks, and whatever other kind of natural litter we could find on the ground. Into them, we stashed hardware items such as tools and wire, flashlights and batteries, lighters, pans, medicine and horse blankets, and anything else we found in the hardware and veterinary cars that we thought might helps us. We even found several tents that we distributed among the lost souls and kept one for ourselves. We didn't feel like thieves for scavenging the stuff from the train because we were in a survival situation and the railroad man had told us to take whatever we needed.

Before the men came back to get the train, we were set up to live in the woods like nomads. We chose places that would be difficult for the authorities to find us and used Dakota pit fires to remain inconspicuous. These are made by digging two holes in the ground a few inches apart with an underground tunnel connecting them. The fire is built in the bottom of one hole, while it is fed oxygen through the other hole. The flame is concealed and they're always built under a tree to disperse the smoke. Aaron showed us how to make them and told us that he had learned it while in a special ops unit in Vietnam.

In the evenings, those of us still living in Swope Park would gather around a communal fire made by Aaron, and he would tell us stories. Sometimes they were Bible stories with Aaron playing the different parts; at other times he told about his various missions in *Nam*. Many times, a few of the mentally ill people would get uncomfortable and leave, but most stayed and enjoyed the entertainment. Sara and I remained the only young people living in the park.

After Aaron tired and went to bed, Sara and I would slip off to our campsite. Every few days, we'd find a new campsite just in case someone was watching us. We were very paranoid about being found, whether by Matthew's gang or by the authorities. Either possibility seemed to hold terrifying outcomes for us. Looking back now, I can see that one prospect was infinitely worse than the other.

We slept in the open most nights that summer, setting up our tent only when bad weather threatened. We slept side by side, though not touching, as the nights were usually hot. Lying night after night next to that beautiful girl, my shell-shocked mind and frozen emotions began to thaw and I felt more alive than I had since my parents' deaths. Aaron said that we, like most of Americans, were probably suffering from Post Traumatic Stress Disorder, or PTSD, like so many of the veterans of foreign wars. Sara was still quite traumatized, I suppose, because every time I tried to touch her romantically, she'd flinch and move further away from me. She always slept with her back to me like she was trying to shut me out. Sometimes, I got so frustrated, I'd have to go off into the woods until I could get myself under control again.

One evening, Aaron went to bed early, saying he had a bad headache and didn't feel like talking to anyone. A lost soul named Patrick decided to take his place as storyteller that night. Patrick was a Vietnam vet also and had always come across as one of the more "sane" ones of the group, even though I could tell that he still suffered from

PTSD like the rest of us. He was quiet most of the time and wasn't prone to muttering or ranting like some of the others, but there was a weariness about him, like he was just tired of living, tired of trying. I think I felt most sad for him because it seemed like he knew what was happening around him, unlike the others, but he didn't have the heart to work very hard at surviving. That evening, though, he became a different person while telling his story.

Like Aaron often did, he told us a story about *the war*. We knew he meant Vietnam, because that was the war that completely changed these men's lives forever; the war that made them lose their sanity or their faith in humanity. I had often wondered what exactly it was about that war that was so unlike the others, but the battles that Aaron and Patrick described were much different than those I'd read about in other wars.

That night, Patrick told us about one mission when his unit was sent to force the *Commies* back across enemy lines. They believed they were chasing a retreating army but instead, ended up outwitted and surrounded by them and swallowed up by the dense jungle. They couldn't see or hear the enemy; they could only sense that they were there, like the hundreds of snakes hanging on the branches overhead or slithering through the leaf litter under their feet. Both adversaries were terrifying, although the tough Marines wouldn't admit being scared to anybody. During the day, the enemy continually fired shots into the clearing where Patrick's unit was trapped, picking off the soldiers one by one. There was never anyone to shoot back at; the enemy was like armed ghosts in the dense jungle. At night, the exhausted Marines tried to sleep in shifts, but the zillion stinging flying insects and venomous crawling ones made one almost wish to be put out of his misery by the Vietcong. *Charlie*, which was what Patrick called the enemy, was often happy to oblige, slipping silently past the sentries and stabbing unsuspecting soldiers as they fitfully slept. By week's end, when the US helicopters finally arrived to liberate them, the Marines were completely spooked and demoralized. As Patrick told the story, his voice became gruffer and his tale more urgent, like it was vital that he get it off his chest.

Patrick went on to describe how his best buddy was killed right beside him one night. It was pitch black and Patrick desperately wanted—needed—a cigarette, but they didn't dare light one up for fear the enemy would spot them and shoot. He and his buddy decided to hide in some bushes and share a smoke under the cover of the foliage, the need for a cigarette being great enough for them to risk their lives, they thought. As they sat and smoked, a knife came whizzing through the leaves, stabbing his friend in the neck. As he lay there gurgling, cigarette still hanging out of his mouth, Patrick grabbed the knife and hurtled it back through the bush in the direction it had come.

Patrick's voice had risen to a shrill, half-crazed tremble. I didn't actually see it when he reached into his waistband and pulled out a big hunting knife and hurtled it toward Sara, but I heard it coming. It seemed like it was traveling in slow motion and in the same slow motion, I thrust out my hand to deflect it. I managed to tip the handle enough for it to just nick Sara's arm before it continued off into the darkness. For a second, I felt all the adrenaline, fear, and torture that Patrick and his fellow Marines must have endured. The whole experience was surreal and frightening.

When Patrick calmed down a bit, after the crazed look faded from his eyes, he was inconsolably sorry he had hurt Sara. He cried and sobbed over her for several minutes while she repeatedly reassured him that she was okay. I wasn't okay, though. All the fear of the night we escaped from the gang hit me like a sledgehammer. I felt that nowhere was safe for us in this crazy new world that Time had forgotten.

Chapter 20
The Beast

The summer came and went with the blur of everyday monotony. Though the days were still warm, at sunset the temperature cooled quickly and darkness fell early. We began to leave the communal fire earlier and sleep in our tent. Even with the dog beds and several blankets, we often woke up shivering and couldn't wait to stoke our ever-burning pit fire to get warm.

One chilly autumn morning—it must have been late September or early October—Sara and I arrived at the zoo to help the keepers for the day. We noticed right away that something wasn't right because the keepers weren't where they could usually be found at that time of day. We also noticed the absence of the lion's occasional roar. We had gotten so used to hearing him roar every half hour or so throughout the day, we normally didn't even notice his plaintive wails, but today, the absence of them was even louder than the roar. It reminded me of how deafening the absence of traffic and sirens was after PF Day when I had lived downtown.

We searched the zoo, starting at the Africa section, because we feared that something was wrong with the lion. He was in his pen looking lazy and satisfied, as a lion should, although he was unusually quiet. Puzzled, we continued searching until we came to the savannah area of the zoo, which sat below the hill from the lion enclosure. From the gate of the savannah land, we could see all five of the keepers crouched down around the body of some kind of antelope. We couldn't tell if it was alive or dead from this far away, but it was obvious that the keepers were frantically trying to do something to it. Not with the slow, measured motions of butchering, but with an urgency that seemed to represent life-saving methods.

We entered the enclosure and sprinted to the group. As we neared, we could tell that it wasn't the large animal they were working on, but a calf that was mewling softly yet plaintively. It and its mother looked like small deer, although I knew from working with them that they were really impala, a species of antelope. We knelt beside the keepers who were pressing bandages against the baby's bleeding flesh, trying to stop the blood loss. They explained that the mother and calf had been attacked by something big with claws and teeth, and we were sickened by the appearance of the mother impala. Her body was torn to shreds and half eaten.

One of the keepers, Jim I think, told me to hold the calf's head so they could try to stitch up its gashes. As I held its head tightly in my lap, it looked up at me, its doe eyes wide with fear and shock, imploring me to help it or maybe just to let it go. It convulsed suddenly, kicking out its legs in all directions and almost striking the keepers with its tiny hooves. Then it slackened, its tongue lolled out, and its head fell back limp on my lap. I watched as the light in its deep moist eyes dimmed and then went out altogether, like someone had turned down a dimmer switch on a lamp. It was the first time I had actually witnessed the death of a mammal and it affected me greatly. I had seen animals and people after they had died, I had killed fish and birds and frogs, I had even been responsible for the deaths of small animals in my snares and traps, but never had a mammal died before me, let alone in my arms. This animal meant nothing to me, yet its death thrust a knife through my heart and I couldn't stop a tear from sliding down my face. I didn't need to be embarrassed, though, because when I looked up, it seemed everyone was affected by the loss of this innocent creature.

We talked about it later in hushed tones like we didn't want anyone around to hear us. The keepers couldn't figure out what animal could have done this. It seemed pretty obvious that it was a big cat, but the lion and the two brother tigers were still in their enclosures, as were the few cheetahs and leopards that were left. The keepers thought it possible that a wild mountain lion had somehow entered the zoo, lured in by the strong odor of dead and dying animals. The ground in the savannah land enclosure was too dry and covered with the hoof prints of panicked animals to distinguish a cat track, so it remained a mystery. None of us could quite understand why the death of this little animal affected us so much more than the hundreds of other animals and thousands of people that had died since PF Day. Maybe it was because we had a chance to save it and couldn't. Or because it had seen its mother get eaten and needed us to fill in the maternal role. Or maybe it was just its innocence, its tragically shortened life.

Whatever the case, I couldn't shake the image of its pleading eyes staring into mine.

I stayed away from the zoo for a couple of weeks after that day, always using excuses like I was tired, or didn't feel good, or that I wanted to do some fishing and hunting to make sure we had enough food for the coming winter months. Sara went without me, never questioning my real motives. I suspected she knew exactly what ailed me, but didn't let on because she knew how much it had bothered me.

One warm autumn afternoon, Sara came back from the zoo to find me filleting my successful catch of catfish and bass to smoke over the fire. I could tell there was something she wanted to tell me, but she was oddly reluctant. Finally she just came out with it.

— *The power's out again.*

I had thought I'd heard some popping noises, but our campsite was at the bottom of a deep ravine and sounds from the outside world filtered down to us muffled and distorted. I had ignored them, just like I usually did. Yet, I couldn't help but be a little curious about it.

— *Does anyone know what happened?*

174

— They think it was another CME. All hell's breaking loose up there again—explosions, fires, panic...

I shook my head and went back to my work. Strangely, this time the power outage had absolutely no effect on me. I told Sara as much.

— Well, I'm glad we're down here, so we're missing out on all the drama.

— You know what this means, don't you?

— No, should I?

— No more electricity—probably forever.

Something in her tone made me look up. I expected to see worry on her face, but instead there was a slight smile.

— No more school, no more institutions, no more running and hiding... We could find a place...

I thought about that for a minute.

— You don't like living here?

— Yes, but winter's coming. It'll be really hard, you know. I'm not sure I'm up to it.

— Maybe the keepers would let us stay with them.

— Maybe... But today they were wondering if it is even worth it anymore.

The zoo will never be open again now. The animals are all going to die eventually. They were thinking about letting the herbivores that are left just run free.

— *What about the carnivores?*

Sara shook her head sadly.

— *I don't know. They kind of avoided that subject altogether.*

It was a desolate thought. Before coming to Swope Park, I hadn't liked animals much, not even cats and dogs. But since coming there and helping to care for them for several months, I felt responsible for them, like they were they were my kids or something. I know the keepers felt the same way, so for them to be thinking of abandoning their charges told me how desperate they thought the situation was. I thought about it the entire evening and lay awake that night wondering what was going to become of the animals and of us.

Chapter 21

Attack

I must have fallen asleep some-time during the night because I was suddenly awakened by the rustling of leaves and the sound of an animal sniffing around outside of the tent right beside my head. It took my eyes a few seconds to open and when they did, I was startled to see the shadow of some big animal right outside the tent. Its hulking body was facing the tent head-on with its snout on the ground. It could have been a bear or a mountain lion or even a huge wild man. I could smell its musky scent when the cold breeze blew our way; I was thankful the breeze was blowing that way so the animal couldn't smell us. I froze, holding my breath so the beast wouldn't hear me breathe.

After a couple of seconds, it made a series of low grunts, then turned toward the back of the tent. I almost gasped when I saw the silhouette of a very large feline looming over the tent. I was suddenly panicked by the memory of the mangled impala and its dying calf. I fervently prayed that Sara wouldn't wake up or make any noise in her sleep and that the predator would find something else to prey on. I was to regret that prayer very soon.

The cat seemed to catch a whiff of something as it raised its snout high in the air. It froze for a second then crouched down into stealth mode. It crept off slowly, gingerly picking its way among the dried leaves in virtual silence. Only after several minutes was I able to move again and quietly woke Sara, holding my finger to my lips to warn her into silence. I think Sara must have been able to see the fear in my eyes by the light of the almost-full moon filtering through the tent, because she was immediately on alert. We scurried to arm ourselves with knives and put on our shoes and coats, just in case.

As soon as we were dressed, we heard a distant growl and then a blood-curdling scream. It sounded like a terrified animal, but soon turned into a man's urgent strangled call for help. Sara jumped up to try to help, but I grabbed her arm and held her back. I was ashamed at my cowardice, but I knew we were no match for a mountain lion or whatever it was out there. Sara didn't care; she threw my arm off angrily and unzipped the tent, leaping through the opening before I could get a good hold on her again. I had no choice but to follow.

The man's screams were lessening as we ran toward the sound, and I knew it must be one of the poor lost souls, who still slept in the open despite the cold and our gift of a tent. After we had run a hundred yards or so, the cat let out a roar that sounded like the zoo lion, though not plaintive and lonely this time, but angry and hurt. We stopped in fear and dread. The roar stopped abruptly at the same time as the man's moans. Cautiously, we approached and what we saw froze us in our tracks.

In a clearing, with the moon shining its ever-smiling face benevolently on the scene, lay the animal, its side heaving with the effort of staying alive. Beside it lay the body of a man, though we couldn't see who it was quite yet. He started moaning again, so I knew he was still alive, but I was afraid to come near to help him in case the predator still had some fight left in him. As usual, Sara had different ideas and started toward him. I caught her roughly and pulled her back, trying to reason with her.

179

— We need to get help. We can't take care of this alone.

— He needs our help now!

— Okay, I'll help him and you go find the others.

I was able to convince her apparently, because she ran off up the hill to where she knew Aaron was camped. If anyone knew how to help, it would be Aaron. I could hear her yelling for him as she scrambled in the loose leaves. My bravado was short lived, though, as I faced the thought of actually going forward to help the poor man. I hesitated until I saw Patrick raise his head and heard him call my name breathlessly. I swallowed my fear and cautiously moved to his side. My heart leapt into my throat when I saw that the predator was indeed the zoo lion and it almost stopped when the lion weakly raised its head and looked me in the eyes. Gone was the glare of the predator I had experienced the first time I visited the zoo, and in its place was resignation. He lay back down with a grunt.

Patrick was clutching a big knife, the one he had thrown at Sara just weeks before. It was covered with blood, as was he himself. It was hard to see where or how he was hurt since there was so much blood. I grabbed his shredded blankets and pressed them to his wounds, trying to stop the blood. His face seemed to be untouched but the back of his head was a shiny black, sticky mess. Between gasps he told me what happened.

— *He got me from behind, Ben. It took me a while to get my knife out to stab him. I got the commie bastard, though! Just like he got Joey.*

I wasn't sure if Patrick knew it was a lion that had attacked him or if he was lost in his memories again, but I tried to calm him down in any case.

— *Yeah, you got him, Patrick. He's dying. You got him good. Now lie still so I can stop your bleeding.*

By the time Sara came back, with Aaron, the keepers, and a few of the lost souls, Patrick had given up. He died happy to have finally defeated the enemy that had haunted his dreams for the last forty years of his life. I didn't cry at his death like I had the baby impala, yet I felt defeated and numb. Patrick was just another life I had failed to save in that miserable year. I wondered when all the death would end. I feared it wasn't about to anytime soon.

Someone had found a policeman, who

somehow had alerted others—they must have figured out a way to communicate when the power was off before—and soon there were several surrounding the lion and Patrick. The lion was still alive, but the keepers and the cops agreed that it should be put down, both because of its condition and the fact that it had killed a man. The keepers seemed sad, but resigned to its fate. Even though Sara believed we would be left alone, we hid while the police were there, just in case.

The next day, several policemen and highway patrolmen came to the zoo to put down the rest of the predators. Everyone knew instinctively that the power might never come back on since all the replacement transformers were destroyed by the second CME and it would take years, maybe even decades to manufacture new ones. The keepers had known the day before that they couldn't sustain the predators of the zoo much longer and had decided among themselves to euthanize them soon anyway. It was a sad day in Swope Park, nonetheless.

After the police left, Sara and I went to the zoo to help the keepers tie up some loose ends. We opened the gates of the herbivores' enclosures. We didn't think they'd survive for long, but we wanted to give them a fighting chance. We were sad that we were forced to leave the primates locked up because even though they weren't normally predators, they still posed a grave threat to people. They had a shot at survival, though, because their enclosures had lots of natural foliage and fruit trees. If they could make it through the winter, they might be okay, but that was rather doubtful. We gathered up all the food we could find and stacked it in their inside areas. Jim and Kyle removed the doors so the animals could not be locked in or out.

The keepers, Sara, and I also inspected the lion's enclosure, trying to figure out how he escaped to carry out his deadly marauding. It took us a while to figure it out, but we finally found a tree limb that had grown a little too long in the direction of the viewing room. He had had to leap a long way, but he was able to span the distance from the limb, over the deep moat that separated his area from the visitor path, landing on top of the viewing room. It made me shutter to think I had been standing there just a few months before, and I had to wonder if my being on the roof had given him the idea to climb the tree and jump over to it.

After the attack on Patrick, Sara and I were afraid to sleep in our tent, even though we knew the lion and all the other predators in the zoo were gone. We couldn't shake the feeling that, but for a different wind direction, we could have been the lion's prey. And we knew there were other predators out there, even in the middle of a big city. The keepers let us stay with them for a few days, but then they decided it was time for them to go back to their homes, if they still stood, and move forward in this new, but already sadly familiar, world.

Chapter 22

Searching

We stayed in the building that the keepers had inhabited for a few weeks, but Sara became adamant about finding some kind of house or apartment to live in now that the power was off again. She said even if we could stay in one of the zoo buildings, she really wanted a bed to sleep in. She reasoned that with so many people having died in the first five months after PF Day, there must be lots of empty places to live. I wasn't sure I wanted to mess with trying to live in a building again; like Aaron and many of the lost souls, I had come to prefer the freedom of living outdoors. Of course, I hadn't tried it in winter yet, and I had to admit that Midwestern winters could be extremely harsh at times. The weather had already been quite cold for living outside.

In any case, my primary concern was to make Sara happy, so one day, she and I walked to the edge of Swope Park where the nice neighborhoods began and started our search for an empty house. It didn't take long. Just two blocks from the edge of Swope Park, we found a house whose windows had been boarded up. As we were poking around it, trying to find a way inside, a man from next door confronted us suspiciously.

— *Can I help you?*

As always, Sara was the one to talk.

— *We were just looking for a place to stay.*

— *Well, you can't stay here. The couple that owns this house is still alive. They're just living with their son right now. And anyway, we don't allow squatters in this neighborhood. It's bad enough with those crazy homeless people always begging from us.*

He shook his head, crossing his arms and staring at us until we left. This was exactly what I'd feared. I was ready to give up and go back to the tent, but Sara had another plan.

— *All we have to do is find an empty house with the owners' names on the mailbox, then make up a story about being their niece and nephew or something. It might take a bit of acting, but I think we*

186

could pull it off.

— *Maybe you could. I'm terrible at acting.*

— *Well, you can just stand there and nod your head while I do all the talking.*

What she didn't add, but I'm sure she meant, was "as usual." We walked around a few neighborhoods, trying to figure out which houses were empty. It was harder than I thought it would be. Without electricity, all the houses looked empty unless we happened to catch a glimpse of someone in a window or outside in their yard. Finally, though, we found another house with the windows boarded up several blocks away from Swope Park.

We cased the house from afar, trying to find out as much as we could about the owners without looking too suspicious. We learned from the mailbox that the owners' names were Dave and Cathy Arnold. The lawn was quite overgrown and had gone to seed, but then so had everybody else's since there hadn't been enough gasoline to waste in lawnmowers since PF Day. We could just barely make out one of those wooden yard decorations featuring the rear end of a plump woman bent over next to a sign. We finally figured out that the sign said

Grandkids spoiled here. We figured that meant that Dave and Cathy were at least middle-aged.

On the walk back to the park, Sara and I discussed our plan. We would go to the house and if anyone confronted us, we would say that we were Dave and Cathy's great niece and nephew instead of their grandkids, in case the neighbors were familiar with the Arnolds' grandkids. We would tell them that our parents had died and that we had walked 60 miles from St. Joseph to live with the only living relatives we knew of.

That evening when we told Aaron our plan, he shook his head and said,

— *I don't think that's such a good idea. People are awful jumpy these days with the gangs and all runnin' loose.*

I agreed with Aaron, but Sara said we should at least try. After all, what could they do to us? Since the second CME there were no phones to call the police and even if the neighbors had guns, surely no one had any bullets left after having to hunt to survive for several months. I reluctantly told Sara we could try her plan the next day.

Aaron shook his head again, muttering *tsk, tsk*. Then all of a sudden he looked up and stared at us intensely over the fire. His eyes looked a little wild in the firelight, maybe angry. When he spoke, he sounded mad.

— *You damn kids never listen. You gonna get us all in trouble, ain't you?*

Then he left the fire and went into his tent. Aaron had been acting strange since the night of the attack. That didn't surprise us, though, as we were all shaken up by it. But now there seemed to be a new dimension to his attitude—anger. Sara felt bad that Aaron was angry with us, but was still determined to try to find a house. She couldn't imagine how us looking for a place to live could have any effect whatsoever on Aaron and the lost souls.

Late the next afternoon, Sara and I went back to the neighborhood of the Arnolds' house. It started snowing lightly as we walked along the empty streets. This time, when we got to the house, we went right up to it like we were supposed to be there. While we were knocking on the doors of the house and trying to peer through the cracks of the boarded up windows, a middle-aged woman called to us from the porch of her house next door.

— *Hey, what are you kids up to?*

189

We walked over to the low hedge separating the houses and Sara answered,

— *We're trying to find our aunt and uncle.*

— *They're not home right now, but they'll be back later. Aunt and uncle, you say?*

— *Yeah, great aunt and uncle, actually. Cathy is our grandma's sister.*

— *Well, like I said, they're not home. You better go somewhere else.*

— *Um, we don't have anywhere else to go. Our parents died and we've walked all the way here from St. Joseph to live with them. We have no one else...*

Hearing the sadness in Sara's voice, the lady came over to where we stood behind the hedge. She looked all around her and said in a hushed tone,

— *Look, I'm sorry you lost your parents and all, but the truth is your aunt and uncle are gone and I can't let you stay in their house without proper legal papers proving you're their rightful heir. The chief of police lives just down the street and everyone is really anxious right now. There was a home invasion last night a couple of streets over and the owners got beat up pretty bad. They said it looked like some homeless person looking for food or something. There's no way the neighborhood is going to allow anybody new in right now. I'm really sorry, kids.*

Sara and I murmured our thanks and walked slowly along the road back to the park. We didn't talk or touch each other the whole way. We were both a little disappointed and disheartened. I didn't think I had wanted to live in a house again until the prospect was snatched away from us.

It was getting dark by the time we made it to the park. The snow was beginning to accumulate and made everything look eerily white in the dim, cloud-scattered moonlight. In the twilight we could just make out the shape of a large vehicle ahead as we rounded a curve in the road. We immediately hid in the trees and cautiously crept closer to investigate. The words *Police* were just visible in iridescent blue letters on the side of the white van. After what we had heard earlier, we knew this could be bad. We also knew we had to warn Aaron and the lost souls as soon as possible, so we headed to the spot that Aaron had pitched his tent for the past few nights.

As we crept toward his campfire, we could hear Aaron talking to someone. Peering from behind a large bush, we saw two cops in uniform standing on either side of Aaron. They didn't appear to be holding on to him, but looked like they were ready to grab him if the need arose. We could plainly hear what they were saying, especially Aaron, who sounded agitated.

— *I haven't done anything wrong and you can't commit me again. I've got my emancipation papers right here in my pocket.*

One of the police officers grabbed Aaron's hand as he tried to reach into his pocket for the papers.

— *We know, Aaron. We've seen your papers before. We're not trying to commit you. We just need information. What do you know about the incident last night?*

— *I don't know nothin'! I was just here mindin' my own business as always.*

— *How many other people live here in the woods?*

— *I don't know nobody else. I just mind my own business.*

— *Now, Aaron, we know you know what's going on. Come on, help us out or we're going to have to take you in.*

— *No! Please don't take me in...*

Aaron's voice had changed from angry

to pleading in a split second. I could feel Sara tense up beside me and knew what she was planning. I grabbed her arm to stop her, but she shrugged me off and went anyway. This was becoming an all too familiar occurrence with us, always ending badly. I had no choice but to follow her into the clearing where the police officers drew their weapons on us. Sara put her arms up and started talking.

— *Aaron was with us all day yesterday. We didn't see or hear anything.*

The cops relaxed when they saw we were just a couple of kids, but did not lower their guns. Aaron began nodding his head like a bobble head doll.

— *That's right, just like I told ya. See? Just like I told ya.*

— *Miss, this is a very serious investigation. We'd like you two and Aaron here to come down to the station with us to answer some questions.*

— *Can't we just do it here? What happened?*

— *No, it's best if we go to the station where we can take your statements.*

— *But we don't know anything.*

— *Yeah, just like I told ya—we don't know nothin'!*

— I'm sorry, Aaron. We still need to get statements from you. As soon as we're done, you'll be free to go about your business.

One of the policemen took Aaron by the elbow and started leading him through the trees toward the street. The other one grabbed Sara's arm. I momentarily thought about running, but the thought of leaving Sara to fend for herself and, even more disturbing, the consideration that she would think I abandoned her, made me lose my nerve, so I allowed the cop to take my arm as well. He led us through the trees to the awaiting police van, where several of the lost souls were already inside.

Chapter 23
Police Station

It felt weird riding in a vehicle after a year of walking everywhere. It was also smelly. Being that close to the lost souls in a confined space was almost more than my nose could stand. Not that I smelled a whole lot better probably, but Sara and I did make an effort to wash ourselves from time to time with water warmed over the fire and dog shampoo that we had taken from the veterinary supply car of the train.

It only took ten minutes to travel the distance from the park to the police station; the same route had taken Sara and me hours when we escaped from Matthew's gang downtown. Sara's eyes got big as a frightened doe's when she realized we were headed to the central police station downtown. I don't think she would have come to Aaron's defense if she knew that was where they'd take us. I had been worried about that all along, because I remembered my dad saying that the central station had been the first to have solar panels installed and the only one to have been completed before PF Day. In my mind, it only made sense that most of the after-dark operations would have to be carried on there, where they could have lights. Unfortunately, I was right.

When we got to the station, Sara clutched my hand as I pulled her close to my side with my other arm around her shoulders. We had to wait in the holding area for a few minutes while they sorted us out. The officers were separating us, sending some to holding cells and others to interrogation rooms.

Sara and I were the last to get assigned to rooms. While we waited, a cop brought in another person. I barely glanced his way, but I took another look when I felt Sara stiffen beside me. It was just an ordinary scruffy looking, bald man, yet I could feel Sara shrinking beside me, trying to melt into my side and disappear. I was about to ask her what was going on, when the man suddenly noticed Sara. He stared at her intently for a second, and then the look turned into a sneer. Right then, I recognized the man as the gang member who had almost found us on the fire escape when we had fled downtown months before.

I had a sick feeling in my gut as a female officer separated Sara and me, placing me in a holding cell. Sara clung to me, pleading with the woman to let us stay together, but the officer gently pulled her away and took her to be questioned. I was left for most of the night in the cell before they came to get me for questioning. By that time, I was so exhausted from lack of sleep and worry about Sara that I don't even remember what the detectives were asking or what I answered. Apparently, they knew they couldn't get any useful information from me because after an hour or so of questioning they sent me back to my cell. I kept asking where Sara was, but they just answered that she was fine, not to worry.

Sometime early in the morning they released me. I begged them to tell me where Sara was, but they just said she had been released a couple of hours before and had left the station. They couldn't tell me which direction she had gone or whether she was alone or not. I exited the building, trying to find familiar footprints in the snow, which had accumulated to about two inches deep during the night. It was impossible. There were so many footprints that the snow was trampled flat in front of the door and much beyond that was covered with the fresh fallen snow.

I looked all around the station in a panic. Where could she be, where could she have gone? Why would she have left the safety of the police station, even if they wouldn't let her stay inside? Why would she leave without me? I strained to look as far as I could down the street to the west. I could see nothing moving except a few small birds picking around in the snow. I looked north and south as well, but still didn't see anything. When I tried to look east down the street, I had to shield my eyes from the rising sun with my hand. It took a few seconds for my eyes to adjust, but then I saw several people standing under an overpass three or four blocks down. Of course! They would want to go somewhere dry to stand and wait for the others to be released. I trotted the few blocks to catch up to them.

As I neared the overpass, though, I could tell Sara wasn't among the men. Aaron was there and several of the lost souls, but no beautiful girl with haunted blue eyes. My heart seized up and I got that sick feeling in my gut again.

— *Have any of you seen Sara?*

Aaron and most of the lost souls shook their heads sadly, but one of them, a disheveled, wild-eyed man named Ernesto, got all agitated, gesticulating wildly with his hands.

— *A demon came and took her. Just swooped in and carried her away.*

— *A demon? What are you talking about?*

I was angry now. I didn't have time for the ranting and delusions of a crazy man.

— *A demon. Or maybe it was Satan hisself... Yes. It was Satan. I'm sure of it now. I think I saw horns on his bald head. He just scooped her up and carried her off. Damn dirty demon...*

At the mention of the bald head, I froze, knowing exactly who he was talking about. I grabbed Ernesto by the shoulders and shook him.

— *Why didn't you stop him?*

Ernesto looked at me incredulously, and then his expression became patronizing.

— *Ain't nobody can stop the devil. Everybody knows that.*

Ernesto shrugged and looked at me pityingly as I dropped my hands from his shoulders. He was right—he couldn't have stopped him and neither could've I. Sara was gone, and I could only hope that the gang would release her, and I would find her unharmed. My voice was quieter but shaky.

— *Which way did they go?*

Ernesto slowly pointed down the street to the west and I took off at a jog, not sure if I was ready to face Matthew's gang, but also not willing to lose Sara to them.

Chapter 24
Grey

I wandered the empty downtown streets all morning, looking for Sara. Everything was grey: the skeletons of the burned-out buildings, the now-useless streets, the piles of dirty snow. I couldn't tell where I was; I may have been going in circles for all I knew because every block looked exactly the same as the last—grey upon grey upon more grey. After what must have been hours, during which my fingers and feet became numb and my throat hoarse from calling her name, I spotted a red pile a couple of blocks away. It looked so out of place among all the grey; it looked so beautiful, like a red flower blooming in the snow. I knew it must be Sara's red wool pea coat, the one she took from her Mom's closet the night we ran away, the one that would make her look older and keep her from being picked up as a runaway. I began running toward her, forgetting all about my tired legs and frozen feet.

As I drew closer, I could see that it was indeed Sara and that she was lying on the ground, her upper body on the sidewalk with her legs hanging over into the street. Her position looked odd, not natural and, thinking she was dead, I struggled to stifle a scream. However, at the sound of my footsteps, she weakly lifted her hand, the one closest to me, so I knew she was alive. When I got to her, I saw that the red was not just from her coat, but also from a pool of blood that she was lying in. It took me a second to realize that it was her blood.

I dropped down and lifted her head onto my lap, murmuring soothing, nonsensical words to her. She opened her eyes and smiled weakly at me, gathering up her strength to speak.

— *They got me, Ben... I tried to give them all the money... but they didn't want it... said it was worthless now.*

— *Shhh, don't try to talk. I'm going to get help. You'll be alright.*

I think I was trying to convince myself more than her. Her eyes looked deep into mine then, imploring me to listen. The haunted look was gone, but in its place was an urgency, a pleading.

— *No... listen, Ben. Remember... re-*

member all I've been saying... all I've been trying to tell you...

— I will, but you'll be alright...

The blood was still oozing through her shirt, soaking into her coat and adding to the pool on the ground. I pressed my hands on her belly, trying to slow the flow of blood, like I had seen the zookeepers do when trying to save the baby impala. Soon the blood was oozing through my fingers and I felt as helpless as I had that day at the zoo, while the innocence and life drained from the poor animal's body. Sara groaned and forced herself to talk through gritted teeth.

— My song... remember my song?

— Yes, If I Die—

I stopped suddenly, tears springing to my eyes, as I remembered the words to her favorite song, *If I Die Young*. Sara continued, but her voice was getting weaker, hoarser.

— I've always known I wasn't going to be here long... I belong with my mom and dad... I was just here to help you... to help you understand... Remember what I've said. Remember, Ben... Promise me you'll remember.

Yes. I will.

I could barely choke out the words; my

throat constricted and my chest felt like it was imploding.

Good.

She smiled then and peace filled her eyes and her beautiful face. She seemed calm and serene like old Mr. Westcott had when they found him dead in his easy chair back in the apartment building. That seemed so long ago, an entirely different lifetime. She seemed to be sleeping for a long time but after a while, she opened her eyes and looked up at me. The love and sadness that radiated from her eyes reminded me of the look that my mom gave me when she opened the watch fob I had given her for Christmas. It was like my life was flashing by in front of my eyes, like I was the one dying instead of everyone I remembered. Then as I watched, the color drained from her face and her eyes slowly glazed over, a dull grey curtain closing over the gorgeous Caribbean blue. I could tell that her soul was leaving her body then. She died staring up at the lifeless grey sky.

— *Sara, no! Don't leave me, Sara! Please! Please... please...*

My panicked words faded into sobs and I sat holding and rocking her for a long time while I cried. I reached in my pocket, thinking about Sara's pocketful of tears, and pulled out Mom's watch fob, still frozen at 11:47 a.m., November 1st. I held it to my heart and screamed at the grey sky, with angry tears spilling down my frozen cheeks. I cried for Sara, I cried for Mom, I cried for Dad, and most of all, I cried for me. Because I was the one left with endless Time stretching before me, Time with no purpose, no happiness, and no one left to love. I cried until I used up all the tears in my pocket and in Sara's pocket too.

After that, I think I fell in a trance or something, not seeing anything even though my eyes were open, my mind a blank. I must have been there for several hours because when I finally came to, abruptly and cruelly, the sun was starting to set behind the grey bones of the buildings to the west. Even the sunset appeared to me in black and white, as if all the colors had been sucked out of the world with Sara's passing.

Suddenly, I looked around me with perfect clarity. My mind felt razor sharp as I took in the scene around me. I could see each dirty grey snow crystal and the ridges of bark on the naked grey tree beside me. I looked down at my lap. Sara's once beautiful but now lifeless grey eyes stared up at me, her skin a lighter shade of grey. The blood pooled around her almost black and gel-like in the cold, the wounds on her body through her shirt—unmistakably knife wounds. The words of Sara's song played in my head, the part about her short life being severed by a sharp knife...

Strewn around her feet were the 100-dollar bills—the Benjamins—she had carried in her pocket for more than a year. They looked grey instead of green. I understood instantly what she had been trying to tell me all along about my dad and his relentless pursuit of money and how, in the end, it was all worthless—worthless and dirty. Money had been worthless to Sara trying to save her life; it was worthless to Mom who had only wanted Dad to spend time with her; it was worthless to Dad, whose grey ashes were mixed in the destruction here somewhere; it was worthless blowing around here downtown like so much trash.

And I knew. I knew what Sara had been saying all along about things not being as they appear. The breakup of my family was never Mom's fault, or even Lyle's. Maybe not even Dad's. It just happened. Dad loved money and me, and Mom loved Lyle and me. And it wasn't Time's fault; it was just life. Life happens, bad things happen to everyone and it is up to each of us to seek truth and happiness and love, no matter what happens. I felt something heavy lift from my body as I opened the treasure chest of memories in my mind and let loose all the old feelings I'd buried for so long. I wasn't happy—far from it—but I was at peace with my past at last.

I watched the sun set as more words from Sara's song ran through my mind, about her thoughts being worth so much more than a penny after she's gone and how people only listen to you after you're dead.

Chapter 25

Dying

I was at peace with my past but I didn't care at all anymore about my future. Without Sara, there was no reason to live at all. Had she actually been in my life or had I just imagined her? Had she been an angel sent to help me deal with my past sorrows and forgive my parents? If so, she had succeeded in that regard, but had ripped open a new wound of pain and loneliness in my soul. I wished with all the broken, shriveled up pieces of my heart that I could die, to be with all the people I loved. Survival, which had been of the utmost importance in my life for the past year, now held no interest for me.

As I sat there on the sidewalk in the snow, cradling Sara's head in my lap, I detachedly considered what I should do next. I remembered the river and my longing to fall headlong into its numbing embrace, but I didn't want to leave Sara's body alone on the street and I didn't have the strength to carry her with me all the way to the river. I also thought about just sitting there, waiting for Sara's murderer to come back and put me out of my misery like a stray dog that's seen too much abuse in its life.

It was dark by then, and I started to think about the nocturnal animals that might start to feed off her. I remembered she hated that everyone always wanted a piece of her—even in death, she would not be left alone—so I half carried, half dragged her body into the nearest ruined building. It had been over 24 hours since I had slept and at least 18 since I had eaten, so I was feeling quite weak. Plus, all the anxiety, adrenalin, and anguish of the past two days had taken its toll on both my body and my mind. I didn't care, though; in fact, I didn't feel anything. I was numb. I knew I should be feeling anger toward the person who killed Sara, maybe plotting some kind of revenge, but I just couldn't bring myself to care. That sounds callous, but at that point I was just ready to die, so nothing mattered anymore.

I laid Sara's body on the soot-covered tile floor of the remains of the building. The first floor ceiling covered a large enough space that I was able to find a dry spot for us. I lay down beside her and drifted off to sleep, hoping beyond hope that I would never wake up again.

Sometime during the night, I heard voices, but I couldn't force myself to open my eyes. I really didn't care who it was or what they were doing there, but at one point, a voice shouted, sounding very near to me.

— *Hey Matthew! I found her!*

The footsteps of several people came near and I tried to force myself to wake up to confront them so they'd kill me, but I just couldn't muster the energy. Instead, I strained to focus on what they were saying and to will them to notice I was still alive.

— *Is she dead?*

— *Yeah, I think so.*

— *Why'd you have to kill her, Grub?*

— *I didn't do it; Zack did.*

— *Zack, you asshole! I told you I could reason with her. You didn't have to kill her!*

Matthew sounded genuinely upset. Like he'd really loved his sister after all. Zack, however, answered flippantly, like he couldn't have cared less.

— *Sorry, man. She fought me.*

Another voice quickly chimed in, sounding excited.

— *How about the boy? He's alive. Ya want me to off him? Just in case...*

Matthew sounded annoyed when he answered.

— *No. Just leave 'em alone. Let's just get out of here, okay?*

I listened dully as the voices faded with their footsteps. I decided that if they wouldn't kill me then I'd just lay there until I died. Maybe Time would be kind to me for once and let death come quickly. Of course, it wasn't.

I don't know how many hours or days passed, but I could feel my body shrinking and shriveling up. Or maybe it was just my imagination, my dreams, that had me dissolving into an insignificant speck. I knew no one was left to remember me or even care that I died; I was but one of millions of innocent souls who had lost their lives to the sun's wrath. Maybe I wasn't so innocent, though. I was wracked with guilt for all the times I was a coward, all the times I turned my back on the people I loved and blamed them for my shortcomings. I begged God for forgiveness and understanding. I was just a kid; did that even matter?

One morning a brilliant light shined in my eyes, forcing me to squint even as my eyes remained close. I tried to ignore the light but it wouldn't let up and I was forced to shift my position. Pain shot through my arm as pins and needles relentlessly stuck my hand. Involuntarily, I sat up in agony, every muscle and bone in my body screaming at me for moving them out of their stupor. I realized that I had been lying for too long in one place. I hadn't died like I'd hoped, and my body told me in no uncertain terms that it was, indeed, still alive.

As I pried my eyes open, a hazy scene came into view and if it weren't for the pain, I'd have thought I was still dreaming. Directly in front of me was a small fire, like a campfire, but made in the basket of a shopping cart, and next to it stood a man. I blinked several times to clear the grit out of my eyes and the man came into focus. He was a young man, maybe in his early twenties, with a scraggly blond beard and torn, dirty jeans. He wore a bright blue nylon parka, which he carefully kept back from the flames. I must have made a sound because he immediately looked over at me with a startled look, and then a smile broke over his face, making it clear up into his kind, light blue eyes.

— *Hey guys! Look who's awake!*

Two other young men, looking to be about the same age as the first, quickly came into focus, bending down to look into my face. The one with curly brown hair spoke to me.

— *Hey, buddy. How are you feeling? We weren't sure you were going to make it.*

I wanted to tell him that was my plan, but my mouth was so dry nothing would come out, so instead I just lay back down and rolled over to my other side. There was some movement and whispering behind me and soon I was gently rolled to my back. Someone sat behind me and laid my head on his lap, while the other tried to get me to drink something. I was too weak to resist.

— *Here, buddy. Drink this.*

I didn't like him calling me buddy. I wasn't his buddy and I wanted nothing to do with the spoonful of warm liquid he was forcing in between my lips. Again, I was too weak to resist, and I choked a little before I could swallow what tasted like a watered-down broth. He wouldn't take no for an answer, however, even when I turned my head to the side. He just pulled my head back around started feeding me again. After a while, my stomach woke up and started grumbling. I groaned and slowly, painfully shook my head no.

— *Come on, buddy. You have to drink it. You need to get your strength back.*

My throat was finally wet enough for me to croak out a response.

— *I don't want strength. I want to die. Leave me alone.*

The first guy, the blond one, knelt next to me.

— *Now, we can't just let you die, kid.*

The one holding my head in his lap agreed.

— *Yeah, you remind me of my little brother. I hope someone is taking care of him back home.*

Suddenly I remembered why I was there and I sat bolt upright, ignoring the intense pain in my head and body. I frantically looked around for Sara, but she wasn't there; had this all been some terrible dream?

— *Where's Sara? What'd you do with her?*

My voice sounded panicked and shrill; the sound was strange to my ears. The guys looked at each other before "Blondie" responded quietly, sadly.

— *It's okay, kid. We took care of her.*
— *What? What'd you do with her?*
— *We buried her. Said a prayer over*

her. She deserved to be taken care of; we couldn't just leave her out for the animals to get at her.

It took a few moments for my mind to comprehend what he'd said, but when I did, I finally slumped back down onto "Big Brother's" lap. "Curly" resumed spooning the broth into my mouth but I just let it drool out the sides and stared listlessly ahead. Sara was truly gone. And I was still here. The cruelness of the situation hit me then and tears sprang to my eyes. I didn't bother trying to stop them or wipe them away but, rather, just closed my eyes tightly and let the tears flow down the sides of my face. I didn't even wipe my nose when it started to leak too, partly from the crying and partly because of the cold. Big Brother held my head and stroked my hair, whispering to me.

— *It's okay, bro. Just let it out. We're going to take care of you. It'll be alright.*

Blondie and Curly got up and went back to the fire, busying themselves with something to let me have some space. After a while, I couldn't cry anymore and I tried to go back to sleep. Big Brother slid out from under me and placed some kind of pillow under my head. And I slept.

Chapter 26
Life After

I awoke sometime in the late afternoon. I sat up slowly, remembering my sore body this time. I was still by the fire, but no one else was around. Slowly, I took in my surroundings. I was no longer in the building where I had lain with Sara. This building was burnt out as well, but three sides were still intact, complete with windows and doors, as well as the ceiling above me. The only open side faced east apparently, as the sun was shining in the windows on the opposite side. The fire in the shopping cart burned near the edge of the ceiling on the east side, its smoke blackening the high ceiling a bit before it made its way out the opening.

I was lying on the floor, which was carpeted with a dirty institutionally-patterned rug, and covered by a thick quilt, its bright colors smudged with soot and stains. Behind my head was a rolled up shirt or jacket of some sort. I carefully, painfully, stood up and looked down at my clothes in disgust. They were filthy and I smelled like the lost souls had in the police van. I winced, the memories of that night and the next morning smacking me in the face and taking my breath away.

Despite the warm sunshine hitting my back through the windows and the fire in front of me, I shivered and moved closer to the fire. Just then, Big Brother came in carrying a load of busted up boards, which he dropped close to the fire. For the first time, I got a good look at him. He was a huge bear-like young man with a thick dark beard and unruly dark hair. His clothes were torn and dirty, just like Blondie's. He wore only a flannel shirt over his jeans.

When he saw me, he looked genuinely pleased and he welcomed me back to the living with a huge smile.

— *Hey, look who's up! How're you feeling, bro?*

I tried to smile back and shrugged.

— *What's your name, bro?*

I didn't feel like talking, but I really didn't like the nicknames these guys were calling me so I squeaked out my name.

— *Glad to meet you, Ben. My name's Dakota. Just make yourself comfortable. We don't have much, but whatever we have is yours to share.*

I nodded at him, happy to be able to call him something other than Big Brother. I tried not to let my guard down, but Dakota's manner was so kind and unassuming, I couldn't help but warm up to him a little. His gentle comfort while I had cried had made an impression on me as well, and I found myself smiling weakly at him despite my resolve never again to make a personal connection with anybody else.

— Doug and Matt are out looking for some food. We'll probably have some more rat stew for dinner. It's their specialty.

Dakota winked and chuckled, and then began stacking the wood, much of which looked like busted-up furniture, on the bottom rack of the shopping cart and stoking the fire inside the basket, presumably to get it ready to cook the delicacy of the day. My stomach grumbled, and even though I had been intent on starving myself to death, I looked forward to the food. I was sickened again by my cowardice; I couldn't even die or starve myself to death when I wanted to. Everyone important in my life had died a heroic death: my dad giving me his food so I would survive; Mom taking care of a sick child; Sara standing up to a murderer. Why couldn't I just refuse to eat, let go of life, and join them?

Before long, Doug and Matt entered the building, laughing and joking. It had been so long since I had heard anyone enjoying life that it sounded alien to my ears. The blond-haired one, which I later found out was Doug, was carrying two fat, dead rats by the tail in one hand while the other hand was holding something behind his back. When he saw me standing by the fire, he grinned and exclaimed,

— Hey! This is cause for a celebration! Good thing I caught this for our dinner.

He pulled a large brown rabbit from behind his back and held it up like it was a prize catch. Well, maybe it was for them. Sara and I had eaten rather well all summer living in the park, but these guys had probably been living in the city proper all this time and had had to make do with whatever little rodents and birds they could find.

The curly-haired guy was named Matt and he had a prize to share as well. In his coat pockets, he had stashed several dandelion plants, which had somehow not only survived in the snow, but had thrived with the extra moisture. Dakota and Doug began dressing the animals while Matt melted snow in a pot set on some kind of grate placed over the top of the shopping cart. He washed the plants in the pot, then threw the water out and melted fresh snow. When the water was boiling, Dakota tossed in cut-up chunks of meat and dandelion. After a half hour or so, the stew was done and Dakota let me eat the first helping from his own bowl and spoon. I was touched again by his kindness.

After we had all eaten our fill, we sat around the fire and the guys told me their story. Somehow they knew not to ask me about mine yet; it was still too raw and painful. Maybe it always would be.

The three had been electrical engineering students at UMKC. They had lived in the dorms until shortly after PF Day when the university had been forced to kick them out. All three were from different parts of the country. They had stayed in Kansas City, living with friends until the power was back on, and then waited around to re-enroll at the university. After the power went out again, they decided to walk to Doug's home in Omaha in the spring, as it was the closest. Until then, they had been living in the buildings downtown, moving every now and then to avoid gangs and the police. They were all very eager for me to accompany them to Omaha, especially Doug.

— *So, Ben, you're coming to Omaha with us, aren't you? You know my family would be happy to have you.*

— *Naw, I'll just stay here.*

— *Do you have family here? Somewhere to go?*

I shook my head, not wanting to give out too much information. My plan was still to figure a way out of my life and the hell it had become.

— *I'll just live downtown here like I have been.*

— *No way, man. We couldn't just leave you here on your own. You're coming with us.*

I knew I wasn't going to go with them, but I didn't feel like arguing, so I just let them think I was. That seemed to satisfy them and they began telling jokes, laughing, and just having a good time. These guys really knew how to enjoy life and make the best of a bad situation. I found myself grinning at some of the crazy things they came up with, despite myself. It had been a long time since I had felt like laughing at

221

anything and the sensation was oddly comforting, even though, at the same time, I felt guilty for enjoying myself.

Matt was an avid fan of zombie movies, books, and all things undead. He was great at telling scary stories that had hilarious twists at the end. He pulled several zombie-apocalypse books and instruction manuals out of his dusty backpack and excitedly showed us various tips and techniques that could be used for general survival, some of which they had already put to use in catching dinner. One device was a very clever small animal trap made out of an old paint can, rubber bands, and some wire. He was able to catch mice, rats, voles, birds, even an occasional rabbit with it.

The devices that warned of an impending attack intrigued me a tiny bit, even though, as far as I knew, none of the casualties of PF Day had as yet come back from the dead to feast on anyone's flesh. One of these used a trip wire and a musical birthday card. Another used one of those personal bodyguard alarms. They also made defensive weapons: a stun gun from a discarded disposable camera, the kind with the flash built in, and another with a cell phone that was useless for communication, yet still had enough voltage to use as a taser. I couldn't compel myself to get interested enough to learn how they were made, however, talking about them was an amusing distraction for my troubled mind.

The longer I stayed with these guys, the less I thought about ending my life. Their interest and zest for life was contagious and I found myself changing my mind about going north to Omaha with them in the spring. I never did tell them my entire story, though. I told them about Dad and Mom dying, but left out the divorce and all the heartache that had brought, because I was at peace with all that.

I know they were probably very curious about Sara—who she was and how she died—but they never pried, and I decided to keep her story to myself. My memories were the only things that I had of her to keep, and I didn't want to share those with anyone yet. The guys showed me where they had buried her, though, in a little urban garden near where she had died. They left me there alone and waited a few blocks away, telling me to yell if I needed them. They had made a grave marker for her out of two pieces of metal, probably taken from the skeleton of one of the burned buildings, tied into a cross and thrust into the ground. I visited her grave a few times that winter; the last time I was there was in early spring, right before we left Kansas City. I found a bunch of purple flowers blossoming inharmoniously in front of the ugly ruins of a building and placed them on her grave. I promised her I'd see her again someday and would think of her shining down on me from heaven every time there was a rainbow.

Chapter 27
The Journey North

Sometime in early April we started our journey to Omaha. We figured it would take a couple of weeks for us to get there, barring any unforeseen circumstances. The guys had two backpacks each and a large duffel bag full of stuff to take. Matt found a discarded metal coffee can and after the guys inhaled the leftover aroma from inside for several minutes like drug addicts snuffing paint fumes, they poked a few holes in it near the bottom and scooped the coals from the fire into it. They poked some holes in the lid as well and placed the can in the bottom of the shopping cart, piling the stack of wood pieces they had scavenged on top. They covered the wood with a raggedy piece of plastic to keep it dry, then stowed the duffel bag and two of the extra backpacks on the bottom shelf and on top of the wood. We each strapped on a backpack and we were ready to go.

I briefly considered taking them back to

Swope Park to get some more supplies from the caches we had buried there and to retrieve my gym bag, but the thought of facing the place where Sara and I were almost happy was just too painful. Plus, I really didn't want to see Aaron and the lost souls and have to explain where Sara was. In the end, I said nothing to the guys about the park, and we began to make our way north through the city.

We skirted the downtown area, hoping to avoid the worst concentration of criminals and police, and instead stayed on the barren interstates. We took turns pushing the cart, but it wasn't long before it got cumbersome. It took a day and a half of almost non-stop walking to make it completely out of the city and to a place with woods a few hundred feet off the interstate where we felt safe making camp and spending the night. It was too hard to get the cart through the underbrush and trees, so we abandoned it at the edge of the trees and carried everything to a clearing where we set up our camp. It was early afternoon, but we were exhausted and cold after walking all night and we wanted time to make sure our camp was safe and would provide shelter should the weather turn bad by morning.

We found the perfect campsite between several big evergreen trees, whose long, thick branches swept the forest floor in a ring around a ten-foot clearing. After sweeping the ground of pine needles, we started a fire with our still-smoldering coals in the middle of the clearing, adding the wood we had brought, branches we found on the ground, and armfuls of dried pine needles, which we found made fantastic tinder. We soon had a nice, warm fire going. Dakota called it a *commanding fire* and we all had to agree that the name fit. I found a creek nearby and started warming some water from it over the fire, while the other guys set animal traps and trip-wire alarms around the perimeter. I gathered some fresh pine needles to make a nutritious tea, and then swept up big piles of needles for our beds under a huge pine tree.

We all decided to hit the sack soon after sunset since we were so tired from our trek out of the city. Sometime during the night, we were awakened by the sound of rain, but we stayed nice and dry under the tree. Luckily, Doug had remembered to gather some hot coals into the coffee can and store them safely under the tree so we could start a fire again. By morning, it was still raining lightly and I showed the guys how to make a pit fire under the boughs of the tree so we could warm up some water for more pine needle tea.

We had gone to bed hungry, as there hadn't been enough time to catch anything in our traps to eat. In the morning, however, we found two squirrels and a plump robin in our traps and snares. It wasn't nearly enough to fill our empty bellies, but it helped ease the hunger pains. The guys tried to give me a bigger share of the food, saying that I was a growing boy and needed it more than they did, but I wouldn't take it. As it was, each of us only got about a palm-sized piece of meat. We even sucked the meager marrow out of the bones of the squirrels. After that, we sat under the tree around our pit fire to wait out the rain shower.

We decided to stay another night in that campsite. The fresh air and nature around us were such a refreshing change after spending most of the winter in the ruins of downtown Kansas City. We were able to trap some more small animals to eat and I found some cattail shoots surrounding a nearby pond. We also gathered a large pot full of young dandelion leaves. After a day of foraging and eating and a good night's sleep, we were refreshed and ready to continue our journey the next morning.

We started out at dawn the next day, deciding to reorganize our packs and leave the duffel bag and shopping cart behind. The bag was full of all kinds of electronic devices, tools, and odds and ends which the guys hated to leave behind. They picked out the best and most useful pieces and stuffed them into the already full backpacks. We each carried one pack and took turns carrying the extra two.

The day was beautiful, sunny and warm, and the walking along the interstate was pleasant. We walked non-stop until late afternoon, passing a few houses and farms just off the highway. When our stomachs started growling and our strength began waning, we decided to stop at one of the houses and ask for food. We chose a big newer home, the kind that company executives used to buy to get away from the corporate grind, thinking that they may have more to share than others. When we approached the house, we heard some people talking around back, so we made our way around the house. A man, woman, and two children were working the dirt in a large rectangle garden, probably getting it ready to plant. They looked up, startled, when we approached. The man confronted us defensively, while his wife and kids hugged each other fearfully behind him.

— *We don't have anything. Please don't hurt us.*

After our initial shock at the family's reaction to us, Doug tried to reassure the man.

— *Sorry to bother you, sir. We don't mean any harm. We're just passing through and wondered if you could help us out. It's okay if you can't.*

— *We just don't have enough to feed us, that's all. We'd like to help you out if we could, but we hadn't recovered from the first PF Day and then the second...*

He shook his head sadly, but still eyed us warily. Doug quickly assured him,

— *Like I said, it's okay. We'll just keep going then.*

We didn't talk for a while. The family's fear unsettled us a little; we hadn't expected that. Maybe they had been the victims of some of the gangs of released prisoners. Or maybe just desperate people searching for anything to cling on to life. In any case, we didn't consider that people living outside the city might have trouble of that sort as well and it made us a little leery about exposing ourselves to the threat of gangs too. We decided to make camp early as far off the highway and into a thick woods as we could.

The next day we made it to St. Joseph, a medium-sized city with lots of nice neighborhoods and homes right off the highway. We tried to beg for food at a few of these homes, but were met with fear, suspicion, and sometimes, downright hostility. One homeowner even met us at the door with a rifle, although it was doubtful he had any bullets to shoot us with. Several people were nice and said they wished they could help us, but everyone was bad off and didn't have anything to spare. When we saw the skinny, sickly-looking children and the sunken eyes and gaunt cheeks of the adults, we completely understood their reluctance to help strangers. After a while, we just quit trying and continued our journey north, camping in the woods between towns and foraging whatever food we could.

The journey stretched out longer than expected since we had to quit walking early every day in order to set our traps, find food and water, and set our perimeter warning devices. I was more grateful than ever that I was with some guys that were not only kind and generous, but were also geniuses when it came to constructing gadgets to keep us safe.

Chapter 28
Trouble

We camped by a pond in a thickly forested area north of the town of Savannah on the sixth day of our journey. Early in the morning, two does and a fawn came to the other side of the pond to drink while we watched in awed silence. After they left, we excitedly talked about how great it would be if we could catch a deer and started thinking about how we could manage that. We knew we'd have to have to have something bigger than the traps and snares we used for small game, so we threw around some ideas using the stun guns and/or knives, but none sounded sufficient to bring down something that large. Still, we couldn't let the thought of a juicy slab of venison go, and we continued to talk about it as we resumed our trek.

Late in the afternoon we passed a farm next to the highway. We could see a man, woman, and two teenagers working out in the field with what appeared to be some old-fashioned farm equipment and horses, presumably planting or getting the field ready to plant. Several minutes later, we passed the farmhouse and thinking that nobody was probably home since they were in the field, we decided to "borrow" some items. We all felt kind of bad about it, but this was survival after all. We were careful not to disturb anything, taking just some hard biscuits, a few potatoes, and some apples. As we were leaving, something shiny must have caught Doug's eye, because he went back in and came out carrying a pistol and a partially full box of bullets. Dakota about had a cow when he saw it.

— *What the hell are you doing with that? You can't just take that!*

— *We'll just borrow it for a while. Maybe we can shoot a deer tonight, then return the gun tomorrow.*

— *I don't know. You're crazy, man. Taking some food is one thing, but a gun...*

— *It's alright. I said we'll return it. They probably won't even notice it's gone.*

We got to thinking about how nice it would be to eat some real meat and to have a full stomach for the first time in a long time, so we finally all agreed to go along with Doug's plan. I think hunger and exhaustion were getting the better of us by then and none of us could think straight.

That night as we camped, we kept hearing animal noises. We could identify the mooing of cows and neighing of horses, and even the occasional crow of a rooster. There were other noises, which we thought might be sheep or goats, but we weren't sure. Since we hadn't seen any deer, we decided to investigate the farm animals and maybe take a few chickens, a lamb, or a goat instead of worrying about trying to catch a deer.

We walked toward the animal sounds and found that they were coming from a nice farm just off the highway. As we hid in the trees, we could see, by the light of an almost full moon, pens of goats, chickens, cows, and horses behind a large, dark farmhouse. Three big silos sat on the side of a gravel driveway between the pens. We started to creep closer to the driveway, but some dogs caught scent of us and came barking. Dakota quickly took some pieces of rabbit meat that he had saved to cook later and threw them to the dogs. That quieted them down and placated them enough to let us into the yard.

We decided that Matt and Doug would take one of the goats and Dakota would grab a couple of chickens, but first I would climb the silo to see if I could get some grain to lure the animals to us. The bottom rung of the ladder to the silo was about shoulder-high to me, so I had to jump up to get my feet on the bottom rung. As soon as I touched the ladder, I knew I was in trouble as an intense pain shot into my arms and through my entire body. The ladder had apparently been rigged to deliver an electrical shock. After that, I lost conscious-ness for a time. The next thing I knew I was being dragged by someone toward the house. I knew I had been caught.

I panicked, my body still tingling and my mind exploding with fear. I was sure that whoever had captured me was going to kill me. I didn't even remember at that point that I had wanted to die; instinct took over and my only thought was that I had to get loose. I started to pull and roll out of my captors' grip, but I wasn't strong enough yet. A few seconds later, a gun was shoved into my face and a woman yelled at me to stop struggling. I was about to give up when a shot rang out and I thought for a fraction of a second that the lady had shot me after all. But the reactions of the woman and the two teenage boys holding me told me that the shot came from the distance. The guys! I heard someone yell and then men shouting.

I gave up then. I didn't even want to face it if one of the guys had been shot. An old man rushed out of the house and he and the woman carried me inside while the boys ran off toward the field where the shot had come from.

They sat me in a wooden chair by the fire and tied my hands in front of me. I had expected them to tie me to the chair or beat me, but instead they tried to make me comfortable. The woman who had held the gun on me looked me over and asked me if I was alright. She was a pretty woman, dark blond hair, probably in her late thirties or early forties. I nodded in response; I didn't trust my voice at that moment and I didn't want to sound like a simpering fool. Besides the older man, there were two older women, grandmas probably, who were looking at me with concern. My mind was still a little numb from the electrical shock and the fear of being caught, so I couldn't figure out why they would be treating me with such care.

Just then a young man and woman came in. The woman—or maybe she was just a girl—was crying and the man was holding his ear, with blood dripping through his fingers. I had a sick feeling in my gut, thinking that maybe Doug had shot at him. That was so uncharacteristic of the usually happy-go-lucky guy I knew, and I couldn't quite wrap my mind around that thought. The first woman—I thought she must be the mother of one of these two—started tending to the bloody ear, and then the door opened again. A man carrying a dog and the two teenage boys came in. The man laid the dog on the coffee table and looked over at me.

— *What's his story?*

The older man answered.

— *He's just a scared and hungry kid, John.*

The man with the dog—John—looked thoughtfully down at the dog for a few seconds, then back at me. His voice was quiet when he replied.

— *Well then, give him something to eat.*

That set off a flurry of activity with the grandmas scurrying into the kitchen like someone had just pushed their "on" buttons. They soon came back with a plate of delicious-smelling food and a huge glass of milk. I tried to refuse it. I didn't deserve their kindness; after all, I had trespassed on their property and tried to steal from them. Yet I hadn't seen this much food—normal-looking food—or even milk for over a year and a half. I fought off the hunger and the desire, but they got the better of me, so I accepted the food with shame in my heart and tears in my eyes. One kind grandma patted my shoulder, but instead of comforting me, it just made me feel guiltier and I couldn't stop the tears flowing down my cheeks.

I was embarrassed and ashamed, but I knew I needed to apologize. I squeaked out an apology, and the woman who patted me smiled kindly at me. Then she turned and said,

— *John, couldn't we untie him now? He doesn't look like he'll hurt anyone.*

John agreed and the older of the two teens came over and untied me. He asked me my name, but when I told them it was Ben, they all looked startled and a little suspicious. I found out later that the dog's name was also Ben and that Doug had shot him as well, luckily just nicking him in the shoulder. The mom—Lauren—made a joke about it being a good thing that the guy was a bad shot, and I couldn't help but smile a little with relief that Doug hadn't seriously injured anybody.

The boy who had untied me told me his

name was Bracken and that I could stay in his room. He gave me some of his clothes to wear and let me clean up a little in the bathroom. I couldn't believe they still had warm running water, although not quite enough water pressure to take a full shower. Bracken told me they had made a solar hot water heater and a special kind of pump to bring water in from the well. After months of sleeping on the ground with just a few blankets to keep warm, I couldn't believe how comfortable the bed was and how warm the house was. Clearly, this family was surviving better than the people living in cities; they had heat, shelter, clothing, plenty of good food, and even running water.

That night, before exhaustion finally took over my brain and body, I told Bracken a little bit about my experiences in the city, leaving out any reference to Sara, of course. I felt like I owed this generous family an explanation as to why the guys and I were trying to steal from them. Bracken seemed to not only understand, but to feel sorry for me. I wasn't sure I wanted anyone to feel sorry for me, least of all the people I had tried to rob.

Right before going to sleep, I asked Bracken what day it was. When he answered

April 13th, I had to smile at the irony. Of course. On my unlucky birthday I almost get electrocuted and my friend shoots an innocent man and his dog.

Chapter 29
Life on the Farm

I decided not to tell Bracken it was my birthday. After the suspicion caused by my name being the same as their dog, I figured the coincidence of it being my birthday was just too great to be believed, so I told Bracken that my birthday was in five days and that I would be turning 16. He offered to teach me how to drive even though there was no gas to get anywhere, and I told him I'd like that. I had no intention of staying there that long, of course, but it made us both feel better to end that awful day on a bright note.

Early the next morning, I crept out of Bracken's room and quietly made my escape. I wasn't sure where I was planning to go, but I hoped to catch up to the guys to make sure they were okay and to continue our journey north. Apparently I wasn't as quiet as I'd thought, because Bracken caught up to me as I was leaving the yard. He grabbed me by the shoulder and turned me around to face him.

— Hey, where're you going?

— I don't know. Just going.

— Why? You can stay here. Don't you want a home to live in?

I thought about that for a moment. What if I couldn't find the guys? What if they had already left the area, thinking I was dead, pushing harder than ever to get to Omaha? I was forced to think about what it was in Omaha that I wanted and it all came down to this, a home, and here was a home—a nice home with a nice family—being offered to me like it was on a silver platter. But why would they?

— Yeah, more than anything. But why would you guys want me? You don't owe me anything.

Bracken sounded perturbed when he answered.

— It's not about owing anybody anything. You need a place and we've got a place. And plenty to feed you too. Besides, you're just a kid. We want you to stay.

I was tired. Tired of arguing, tired of traveling, tired of trying to survive. What Bracken offered me was so tempting, but I was also scared. I had promised myself not to get close to anyone, but I could see myself really getting close to this family. I longed for a mother and a father to take care of me. I longed for doting grandparents to love me unconditionally. I realized that I was jealous of Bracken, of his life and his family. I wanted it so badly, but I was scared of losing everything again. I started crying tears of longing, of sadness, and of shame. Bracken pulled me close and comforted me and I craved that closeness, the acceptance that the guys had given me. If they were indeed gone, maybe I could find it with Bracken, and everything else I desired here with his family. Finally, I gave up and let Bracken lead me back inside.

Later that morning, while I savored a delicious breakfast and watched this happy family who seemed almost oblivious to the hardships of much of the rest of the world, I began to worry about the guys. What if one of them was shot and was lying out there, bleeding to death? The guys had become like older brothers to me and I knew they were kind and generous, really good people. I was scared to bring up the subject, though, worried that the bad feelings Bracken's family held for Doug would spill over to me and I'd be kicked out of the house. Maybe that would be better, I thought. Maybe I deserved to be. So I decided to ask.

— *Do you think you shot any of the guys I was with last night? I just don't want them to be lying out there bleeding to death. They're really not bad guys; they took care of me after my parents died.*

John, the dad, looked a little pissed off, but he answered nicely enough.

— *Well, they ran off and left you hanging there. But don't worry; we shot over their heads. We just wanted to scare them off, not hurt them. Alex and I'll go down there and check around later just to be sure.*

Alex was Bracken's older brother, the one whose ear had been shot, and the pretty girl with copper-colored hair, who had been clinging to him the night before, was his wife, Robin. They made a cute couple and were pretty nice to me even though I had caused them so much pain and heartache.

Later in the day, two cute girls rode up to the house on horses. I had never been so close to a horse and I had certainly never ridden one, but one of the girls, named Jenny, let me ride double with her. The weather was warm and sunny, the girls good company, and for a while I was able to mask the pain in my heart and bury the haunting memories of the city. It was almost like that part of my life had been a dream and I was just now waking up to reality. My old nemesis Time decided to play nice and let me enjoy the afternoon, stretching it out slowly and deliciously, so I could pretend to be happy and normal for a while.

Bracken's girlfriend, Skylar, was a beautiful girl about the same size that Sara had been, but with light brown hair. Something in the way she talked and looked at Bracken reminded me of Sara, and I realized that I kept staring at her longingly because every time I did, Bracken would glare at me. Later that night, Bracken warned me off her just in case I didn't understand that she belonged to him and that he intended to marry her. I hadn't meant to threaten their relationship or to steal her away from him. It's just that I felt myself drawn to her like hapless waves to a comforting shore. After that, I made more of an effort to control my emotions when I was around her.

For the next two weeks, I tried to fit in to the family, helping with household chores and various farm projects. I tried to please Lauren and John to show them my gratitude and that I was worth their trouble, but when they weren't around my heart just wasn't in it. They reminded me of my parents and I so desperately wanted a relationship like that with them, but I knew in my heart it would never be the same; that stage of life was over for me now. I had been too long without parents to care for me; my heart felt hardened and crusted over, too rigid to allow anyone new in. Especially these good, happy people who had no clue what I had been through and could never understand the damage that had been done to my heart.

One day I was out walking the fence line with Bracken and his younger brother Calvin. I tried to keep my mind focused on the task, but it just kept fogging out, making it impossible to stay focused. I don't know what was wrong with me; I felt like my mind was shriveling up even as my body began to fill out from the good food. Bracken kept telling me to keep up. I tried my best, but it just wasn't good enough; I lagged behind the others.

At one point, I passed a large clump of bushes. I was almost past when I heard my name softly called through the bushes. It took me a second to realize it was Dakota and another few seconds to figure out what to do. I told Bracken and Calvin that I had to take a leak, and then disappeared into the bushes.

I was so happy to see all three guys hiding deep in the bushes, and they were apparently elated to see me. They hugged me so hard I almost passed out. They were whispering excitedly, Dakota with tears in his eyes, exclaiming that they had thought I was dead when they ran from the farm and were overjoyed when they heard from Jenny and Skylar that I was alive and well. They explained that after secretly returning the fateful gun to its owners, they had sought refuge in the nearby town where Skylar and Jenny happened to live. It seemed that fate had brought us back together and I decided that I'd leave with them later that night. At least with these guys I didn't have to pretend to be interested in life and the mundane things that go along with living. They understood what I'd been through and didn't try to push or pull me into being something I just didn't have the strength to be anymore.

Late that night, after everyone in the house had been asleep for several hours, I slipped out the back door and met up with the guys by the fence. I had taken some bread and a few slices of ham to placate the dogs so we could make a quiet getaway. As

I climbed the fence, I looked back at the sleepy house, so pleasant and unaware of the hell that the sun had unleashed in the cities. On this farm, Time had plodded along almost like nothing at all had happened. I was tempted to stay, but I felt I could never fit in with the peace and happiness it contained.

Chapter 30
A Home and a Purpose

The guys had moved into an old abandoned home on the edge of the small town about a half-day's walk from Bracken's farm. Unlike in the big city, the neighbors had allowed the guys to live in the house as long as they took care of it and until the deceased owner's heirs came to claim it. Even the town's one police officer condoned the deal, but he warned them that any "funny business" would get them promptly run out of town.

The house was a nice two-story Victorian home about a quarter mile beyond the last house in the neighborhood. It was surrounded by fields, which had been overgrown with weeds and the occasional volunteer corn plant. The kitchen was large and comfy, and the upstairs had enough bedrooms so that we each got our own. Best of all, according to the guys, who eagerly gave me the tour, was the huge garage/workshop, which was full of equipment, tools, two large workbenches, and plenty of windows to let in natural light. It had a woodstove in the corner for heat and even a skylight over each workbench. Ideal, they said, for inventing. There was a cistern out back that was nearly full of water. We had to carry it in with buckets and boil it for drinking, but it was readily available, at least for now.

Every day, the guys and I went into town looking for chores we could do to earn food and parts from lawnmowers, electronics, etc. At first, the guys kept their invention ideas a secret even from me, but eventually they showed me their designs. As soon as they gathered enough parts, they began working on them. They couldn't wait to get back home everyday with their new acquisitions. Since I knew almost nothing about electronics, inventing, or physics, and my math skills were pretty weak, the guys patiently explained and demonstrated things to me, allowing me to apply what I'd learned on extra pieces of equipment.

All of the things the guys and I were working on had to do with making life easier for people. We rewired solar arrays and small wind turbines, which had been damaged during the CME's, into well pumps and heat exchangers, took apart lawn mowers and made them into generators to run emergency equipment and power tools, and fashioned small electrostatic motors out of recyclables. We also made heat exchangers out of wood and empty pop cans and traded them for food at the market that was held in the school gymnasium. Many of the items we gave away free to desperate families in need of heat or a source of power.

Another type of project that the guys and I worked on and used for bartering was a defense system for people's farms. With the help of Matt's zombie manuals, we showed farmers how to make weapons out of things they could find around the house, and how to set up a perimeter alarm system to warn of marauders, which were beginning to be a serious problem. Doug still felt bad about wounding Bracken's brother and dog, so we helped their family with a defense system for free to help make up for it. They accepted the apology and help graciously.

The guys had a top-secret project, which they were most excited about and worked on late into the night, relying on light from candles at first, then from some of our solar and generator projects. Using odds and ends like glass bottles, PVC pipe, copper wire and tubing, aluminum foil, and the transformer from a neon sign, among other things, they were able to fashion a high-voltage Tesla coil, capable of generating electricity. They worked for months perfecting it and making it safe for everyday use in households. Since my math and science skills were still lacking, but my penmanship and drawing abilities were fair, the guys had me write all the notes and draw illustrations and diagrams of their work. I became adept at writing coherently, and even noticed that my vocabulary and grammar improved greatly the more I was around the three highly intelligent geeks I had come to love as brothers.

I dated Jenny Garten, Skylar's friend, for several months after moving to town, but she developed an interest in Matt and started dating him instead. I didn't have a problem with that; she was too flighty for me. On the other hand, she suited Matt's crazy-fun personality perfectly.

I met a girl in town named Taylor Smith, with whom I have found a comforting affinity. Like me, her life has been full of heartache and sorrow, and Time has not been kind to her. Most of her childhood was spent being shuffled from one relative to another while her parents alternated between drug and alcohol binges, jail, and rehab. Her older brother Irvine, who had been in Bracken's class at school, had also fallen into the abyss of drug addiction. Taylor felt like everyone who was supposed to take care of her had abandoned her. Shortly after PF Day, her parents were released from jail and tried to make a family for her and Irvine. Unfortunately, without drugs or alcohol to feed their addictions, they and Irvine became alternately volatile and angry, then sullen and depressed. Taylor tried to be placating or simply stay out of their way, making herself as inconspicuous as possible, but Irvine often fought bitterly with both his parents. Soon they had kicked Irvine out of the home and he was later found frozen to death in the town park after a snowstorm. Taylor has never gotten over his death or her parents' abandonment of her, just as I have never gotten over my losses. But I have learned some things since coming to this quaint little town.

As I come to appreciate this new life and the purpose I have found, thanks to my brothers, helping people survive and thrive in this world that Time has forgotten, I have realized several things. One is that money, or whatever is substituted for money, is worthless unless you have loved ones to share it with, to really be with and appreciate. Another is that, like Sara always said, life isn't always what it seems; one should always try to look at an issue from all sides before jumping to conclusions and passing judgments. And Time, which I used to think was my enemy, is simply the means by which we measure our successes and failures in life; those, in turn, influence how fast or slow we perceive Time to be passing.

Finally, survival isn't just about knowing how to forage for food, or find shelter, or protect yourself from all the bad things that life throws at you; it's about figuring out how to find happiness and love, how to move beyond the bad things and search out good stuff, and ultimately, how to make a new life, a life with purpose and relationships, the things that make a life worth living. I'm happy to say that I'm almost there. I've come to terms with my anguished past, established a sustainable present, and am looking forward to a future with limitless possibilities.

There's only one thing I hold near and dear to my heart, and that is my Sara. Maybe someday I'll tell Taylor and the guys about her. Or maybe I'll just keep her memory tucked away in my pocket to replace those tears I spent the day she died. I'll hold her memory next to my mother's watch to remind me never again to waste the Time I have been gifted with the people I love.

Discussion Questions

1. What were some of the themes throughout the story? How did those themes affect the story and help move it along? (Examples: time; money—Benjamins; the number 13; color—the blue of Sara's eyes, her red coat, the grey surroundings when she died, etc.)

2. Ben felt like Time was his enemy through most of the story. At what point did his perception of Time begin to change and when was he able to come to terms with it?

3. How would you describe Ben's personality? Is he shy, sensitive, and introverted or outgoing and gregarious? Does he confront problems head-on or try to avoid thinking about them? How does his personality type help to shape the story?

4. What did Aaron mean when he said, "Well now. Emancipation is something I know a little bit about"?

5. Why did Aaron call the homeless people in Swope Park "Lost Souls"?

6. Why did the Lost Souls prefer to live in the park instead of some of the many empty buildings and houses?

7. Why did Patrick hurl the knife at Sara?

8. What was the significance of color when Ben found Sara dying?

9. Why do you think both old Mr. Westcott and Sara have peaceful expressions on their faces when they died?

10. Why did Doug "borrow" the gun from the empty farmhouse?

11. How did Bracken's family's perception of Ben's personality differ from Ben's reality? (If you've already read *How I Became a Teenage Survivalist*.)

12. Ben felt like he couldn't stay with Bracken's family. Why is that? Why did he feel more comfortable living with his three friends?

13. What are the things Ben learned about life by the end of the story? How can you apply these words of wisdom to your own life?

Find Out More

"Our sun is approaching a period of high turbulence, referred to as the solar maximum, with many scientists suggesting a peak in activity around 2013." This activity could result in a solar superstorm which, under the perfect circumstances, could cause the collapse of the power grid as portrayed in *TIME LOST: Book 2 in the Teenage Survivalist Series*.

Find out more about solar superstorms and coronal mass ejections (CME's):

NOVA Secrets of the Sun
http://www.pbs.org/wgbh/nova/space/secrets-sun.html

The Sun's Wrath: Worst Solar Storms in History
http://www.space.com/12584-worst-solar-storms-sun-flares-history.html

NASA Science: A Super Solar Flare
http://science.nasa.gov/science-news/science-at-nasa/2008/06may_carringtonflare/

Solar Superstorm Could Knock Out US Power Grid
http://www.reuters.com/article/2012/08/04/us-solar-superstorm-idUSBRE8721K820120804

Learning how to survive without electricity is all about creative problem solving. Think about everything in your life that runs on electricity and try to figure out a way to replace each of them. The links below show how Ben and Sara solved some of their most pressing problems.

Find out how to become a survivalist:

Surviving An Urban Disaster: Interview With Richard Duarte
http://www.offthegridnews.com/2013/06/12/surviving-an-urban-disaster-interview-with-richard-duarte/

Urban Survival Tips - Part 1
http://urbansurvivalsite.com/urban-survival-tips-part-1/

Urban Survival Tips - Part 2
http://urbansurvivalsite.com/urban-survival-tips-part-2/

Scavenging For Survival
http://uscrow.org/2013/05/12/scavenging-for-survival-after-shtf/

How to Turn a Pallet into a Garden
http://www.onehundreddollarsamonth.com/update-how-to-turn-a-pallet-into-a-garden/

About the Author

Julie Casey lives in a rural area near St. Joseph, Missouri, with her husband, Jonn Casey, a science teacher, and their three youngest sons. After teaching preschool for fifteen years, she has been homeschooling her four sons for ten years. Julie has Bachelor of Science degrees in education and computer programming and has written four books. She enjoys historical reenacting, wildlife rehabilitation, teaching her children, and writing books that capture the imaginations of young people.

Find out more at www.julielcasey.com.

A Message From the Author:

Thank you for taking the time to read my book. I would be honored if you would consider leaving a review for it on *Amazon*.

I'd like to shout a big thank you to all my family, friends, and fantastic supporters of the Teenage Survivalist series.
You all are the best!

Check out these titles from
Amazing Things Press

Guardians of Holt by Julie L. Casey

Keeper of the Mountain by Nshan Erganian

Rare Blood Sect by Robert L. Justus

Evoloving by James Fly

Survival In the Kitchen by Sharon Boyle

Stop Beating the Dead Horse by Julie L. Casey

In Daddy's Hands by Julie L. Casey

Time Lost: Teenage Survivalist II by Julie L. Casey

Amazing Things Press

www.amazingthingspress.com

Made in the USA
Charleston, SC
28 March 2014